THE
HIGHBINDERS

D0013281

MATT BRAUN

St. Martin's Paperbacks

This is a work of fiction. All of the characters, organizations, and events portrayed in this novel are either products of the author's imagination or are used fictitiously.

THE HIGHBINDERS

Copyright © 1984 by Avon Books.

All rights reserved.

For information address St. Martin's Press, 175 Fifth Avenue, New York, NY 10010.

ISBN: 978-0-312-99784-7

Our books may be purchased in bulk for promotional, educational, or business use. Please contact your local bookseller or the Macmillan Corporate and Premium Sales Department at 1-800-221-7945, ext. 5442, or by e-mail at MacmillanSpecialMarkets@macmillan.com.

Printed in the United States of America

Avon Books edition / March 1984
St. Martin's Paperbacks edition / July 2004

St. Martin's Paperbacks are published by St. Martin's Press, 175 Fifth Avenue, New York, NY 10010.

10 9 8 7 6 5 4 3 2

TERROR ON THE RAILROAD

The sky was suddenly lighted by an earsplitting blast. The force of the explosion instantly transformed the railway yard into a tangled mass of steel and wood. A towering ball of fire leaped skyward and the concussion shook the earth. A billowing cloud of smoke rose from the devastation, blotting out the moon.

Tallman lay flattened out on the roof of the boxcar. He stared at the distant flames and concluded that some combination of nitro and dynamite had been used in the bombing. Then he heard laughter and shouts from inside the boxcar, and realized the bombers were congratulating one another on a job well done. He wormed to the other side of the boxcar and found a handhold on the roof. Feet first, he lowered himself over the edge and swung through the open door. He landed on his knees and rolled, drawing the Colt.

"Don't move!" he ordered, rising to one knee. "I want you alive!"

Porter and Cobb were framed in the opposite doorway. A split second elapsed. Then both men pulled their guns…

"Braun blends historical fact and ingenious fiction…a top-drawer Western novelist!"

—Robert L. Gale, Western Biographer

ONE

Tallman stepped down from a hansom cab. He paid the driver and stood for a moment at curbside. The morning was bright and sunny, and Washington Street was crowded with passersby. He tipped his hat to an attractive woman and smiled as she peeked at him from beneath her parasol. Then he walked to the arched entranceway of an imposing, four-story brick office building only a few blocks from Chicago's Loop.

Tallman entered the lobby and mounted a flight of stairs. On the second floor, he moved briskly along the corridor, halting before a suite of offices. The upper half of the door was frosted glass, emblazoned with gilt scrollwork. The name of the firm stood out in bold relief.

PINKERTON DETECTIVE AGENCY
Allan Pinkerton
President

With a jaunty smile, Tallman entered and swung the door closed. The reception room was utilitarian in appearance, with one leather sofa and a lone desk. A large inner office was directly opposite the door, and several smaller offices were ranked along an adjoining hallway. The receptionist was a pert blonde, with Kewpie doll features and a passable figure. She looked up from the desk and suddenly sat up straighter. Her hand fluttered to her hair.

"Good morning, Mr. Tallman."

"Good morning, Myrna." Tallman doffed his fedora gallantly. "You're looking radiant, as ever."

"Oh, Mr. Tallman!" Myrna batted her lashes. "You shouldn't tease a girl that way!"

"On the contrary," Tallman said, grinning. "Whenever I come here, you brighten my entire day."

Myrna smiled engagingly. "Perhaps you don't come here often enough."

There was open invitation in her tone. Women were attracted to Ashley Tallman's animal magnetism and the underlying promise of conquest. A man who fitted his name, he was tall and handsome, with sandy hair and the lithe, muscular build of an athlete. His rugged features were dominated by a determined jaw and steel gray eyes set deep under a wide brow. His character was forceful and charming; he was a ladies' man whose very presence inspired respect in other men.

Today, he was attired in a dark gray single-breasted suit, with a pearl gray fedora and a matching four-in-hand tie. The combination was at once striking and conservative, and somehow made his eyes all the more piercing. He gave the girl a slow once over.

"Careful, Myrna," he said in a suggestive voice. "You might tempt me too far, and the boss wouldn't like that. He's a stickler on the proprieties."

Myrna giggled. "What he doesn't know won't hurt him . . ."

"Who's teasing now?" Tallman said with a wry smile. "Don't bother announcing me—I'm expected."

Myrna watched with a vaguely deflated look as he crossed the reception room. He hooked his fedora on a halltree, then rapped once and stepped through the door into Pinkerton's inner sanctum overlooking Washington Street. The office was furnished with leather armchairs and floor-to-ceiling bookcases; behind a massive walnut desk sat Allan Pinkerton. He was stocky and thickset, with a full beard and a shock of salt-and-pepper hair. His face was reserved and stiffly formal.

"Come in, Ash." He pulled out a pocket watch. "You're an hour late."

"Why spoil a record?" Tallman seated himself in an armchair.

"Humph!" Pinkerton regarded him dourly. "I sometimes wonder why I tolerate your insubordination."

"Simple," Tallman said with cheery vigor. "You're afraid to fire me. I might open my own agency."

Pinkerton seemed undisturbed by the thought. Some twenty years ago, shortly after he'd emigrated from Scotland, he had founded the detective agency. Throughout the Civil War he and his operatives had served as spies and espionage agents for the Union Army. These wartime exploits had won the agency a nationwide reputation for undercover work. Following the end of hostilities the firm had expanded into the protection of banks and railroad express cars. There was no federal law enforcement, and local peace officers were hindered by poor communications and vast distances. As a result, the agency served as a watchdog for business and industry. Allan Pinkerton and his agents were looked upon as America's guardians of law and order.

Still, Pinkerton had no wish to lose the services of Ash Tallman. In the latter stages of the war, Tallman had been recruited for clandestine missions behind Confederate lines. Then, with the coming of peacetime, he'd stayed on as a Pinkerton agent. He was something of an actor—a master of disguise—and was considered the top undercover operative in the business. There was a fine line past which the government and law enforcement, not to mention the private sector, could not take legal action. So Tallman's assignments were often quasi-legal, and inevitably dangerous in nature.

Then, too, Tallman was unique among the agency's operatives. There was nothing in his debonair manner to suggest deadliness and cold nerves. Yet he'd killed five men in gunfights, and in moments of stress he exhibited the steely inner discipline of a blooded veteran. His fellow agents, never easily impressed, were of the opinion he ate nails for breakfast and pissed ice water. And Allan Pinkerton overlooked both his carefree attitude and his excesses with women. Ash Tallman was indispensable simply because he was a survivor. He never balked, no matter how hazardous the assignment.

"Someday"—Pinkerton paused long enough to lend emphasis to the word—"someday you will go too far and force me to dismiss you."

"Not a chance," Tallman replied genially. "Deep down, you think I'm a prince of a fellow." He chuckled softly.

"Spare me your wit." Pinkerton snorted testily. "I sent for you to discuss a new case. Your assignment starts today and I would appreciate your undivided attention."

"I'm all ears," Tallman remarked with impassive curiosity. "Who's the client?"

"The Southern Pacific Railroad."

"California?"

Pinkerton nodded. "The San Joaquin Valley."

"Train robbers?"

"No," Pinkerton informed him. "Squatters."

"Squatters?" Tallman looked genuinely surprised. "I thought we limited ourselves to criminal investigations."

"We do." Pinkerton steepled his hands and tapped his forefingers together. "In this instance, we've been retained to expose a criminal conspiracy."

"A conspiracy involving squatters?"

"To be more precise," Pinkerton noted, "it involves an organization of squatters. They call themselves The Settlers' League."

"Settlers and squatters aren't exactly the same thing."

"Perhaps we should begin at the beginning. Immediately after the war, as you will recall, the government awarded several million acres in land grants to the railroads. The Central Pacific and the Union Pacific linked up to form the transcontinental line. In addition, the Southern Pacific built southward through California. Those are the lands in question."

Tallman fixed him with a steady, inquiring gaze. "And, squatters have illegally taken possession of land awarded to the Southern Pacific. Is that the gist of it?"

"Exactly." Pinkerton indicated a letter lying on his

desktop. "I have here a communiqué from Otis Blackburn, General Superintendent of the line. His concern centers on certain parcels located in the San Joaquin Valley."

"Have the squatters filed for title under the Homestead Act?"

"Not according to Otis Blackburn."

"How long have they occupied the land?"

"I have no idea," Pinkerton admitted. "Blackburn made no mention of it in his letter. Nor do I find it particularly germane to the case. Squatters are squatters . . . and conspiracy is a criminal offense."

"What kind of conspiracy?"

"A year ago," Pinkerton explained, "the Southern Pacific brought suit in federal district court. The court upheld the railroad's position and ordered the squatters to vacate the land. The Settlers League then entered an appeal to the Supreme Court. No decision is expected until the fall term."

"Why not wait until the court rules one way or the other?"

"The Southern Pacific wants them off the land *now*."

Tallman met his stare levelly. "So far, I haven't heard anything that sounds like a conspiracy."

Pinkerton's face grew somber. "Within the past month, several acts of sabotage have occurred. Tracks were removed in an effort to derail trains. Bombs were planted to destroy a locomotive and nearly a dozen cars of rolling stock. Only last week a bridge was blown up over the King River. In short, the Southern Pacific is under siege."

"Any hard evidence to connect the sabotage to the Settlers' League?"

"Nothing concrete." Pinkerton frowned and shook his head. "Apparently the squatters fear an adverse ruling from the Supreme Court. By engaging in guerilla warfare, they clearly hope to force the railroad into an out-of-court settlement. The end result—unless they're stopped—would be negotiation by terrorism."

Tallman deliberated a moment. "How many squatters are there?"

Pinkerton's frown deepened. "Numbers are irrelevant. The sabotage campaign has received widespread publicity. People are justifiably frightened, and land sales to new settlers have all but dried up. The overall effect has been to place the Southern Pacific in a ruinous financial position. Which brings us back to the central issue—the League must be stopped!"

"Does Blackburn's letter give any specifics on the League itself?"

"Quite obviously, they are a mob of anarchists. As to specifics, you are to report directly to Blackburn. He will brief you on the details of the case."

"When do I leave?"

"Tomorrow," Pinkerton advised. "Leland Stanford, Southern Pacific's president, has dispatched his private car for your trip to San Francisco. I am informed it will arrive here tonight."

"Sounds like he's in a hurry to get me there."

"I cannot stress the urgency of your mission too much. Every moment of delay further jeopardizes our client's position."

"How do you want the investigation handled?"

"Undercover," Pinkerton ordered. "Your first objective

must be to infiltrate the League and gather evidence of a conspiracy."

"And then?"

"Secure criminal indictments against the League's leaders. With them in jail, the League itself will collapse."

Tallman considered briefly, then nodded. "I take it the Southern Pacific will then evict the squatters—before the Supreme Court ruling."

"Oh, indeed," Pinkerton said with a hard grin that had no mirth to it. "After all, possession is nine points of the law."

"So I've heard," Tallman said equably. "Anything else, or does that cover it?"

"One other matter we haven't yet discussed."

"What's that?"

"Miss Valentine." Pinkerton peered at him like a stuffed owl. "Are you planning to use her on this case?"

"I believe so," Tallman said with an odd smile. "Vivian's a natural for our business."

"Perhaps," Pinkerton said, arching one eyebrow. "Tell me how her training has progressed."

Tallman delivered a brief report. The lady in question had a checkered past. On a previous assignment, Tallman had infiltrated a confidence ring in New York City. One of the gang's members was an auburn-haired beauty named Vivian Valentine. A professional bunco artist, she had played the Big Con in several cities along the eastern seaboard. After breaking the case, Tallman convinced her to turn state's evidence in exchange for immunity. He then persuaded Pinkerton to recruit her into the agency.

Curiously, he'd encountered little resistance from

Pinkerton. However hidebound in some ways, the agency chief was remarkably liberal in his views toward women. Shortly before the Civil War, Pinkerton had hired the first woman detective in the nation's history. Her name was Kate Warne, and she had served with distinction as a Union spy. Following the war, until her death in 1869, she had performed brilliantly as an undercover operative. So Pinkerton was not averse to recruiting another woman into the agency. His sole condition was that Tallman accept responsibility for her training and her conduct. He wanted assurance that Vivian Valentine would indeed go straight.

The probationary period had been set at one month. As Tallman explained it now, Vivian had proved herself an apt pupil. With her background as a bunco artist, she was perfectly suited to work involving subterfuge and guile. He'd further honed her talents and instructed her in the art of disguise. In terms of training, he expressed the opinion that Vivian had learned all there was to be learned in a classroom atmosphere. It was time now to put her to the test, and observe her under fire. In short, he thought she was ready for a field assignment.

"We'll make a good team," he concluded. "She's quick and foxy, and we think alike. Those are the things that count when you're working undercover with a partner."

"Very well," Pinkerton agreed. "I trust your judgment, Ash. If you're satisfied, then I have no objections."

"Vivian will be pleased to hear it."

"However, I would remind you of one thing. In the field, your life will rest solely in Miss Valentine's hands. A single error on her part might very well get you killed."

Tallman laughed. "Are you worried about my life or the assignment?"

"Both, of course." Pinkerton nodded and smiled benignly. "Just complete your assignment and come back in one piece."

Tallman uncoiled from the chair and got to his feet. After a warm handclasp, he turned and walked to the door. There he paused and flipped Pinkerton a salute. Then his mouth curled in an urbane smile.

"Wire the boys in Frisco," he said, stepping through the doorway. "Tallman and company are on their way."

TWO

The sun went down over the mountains in a great splash of orange and gold. Tallman was seated in an over-stuffed armchair, staring out the train window. His expression was abstracted, and a black panatela cigar was wedged in the corner of his mouth. His eyes were fixed upon the distance.

The train chugged slowly toward the summit of the High Sierras. Behind lay the winding canyon of Truckee River, and ahead the mountaintops were still splotched with crusty patches of snow. The altitude topped 7,000 feet, and far below was a spectacular view of Donner Lake surrounded by wooded mountain slopes. Across the summit, the fifty mile descent from the Sierras was almost straight down. Tomorrow morning, after highballing around switchbacks and thundering over sheer gorges spanned by bridges, the train would arrive in Sacramento. From there, it was a pleasant one-day journey to San Francisco.

For the past three days Tallman had been traveling in style. The private railroad car was both spacious and lux-uriously appointed. The arched ceiling was adorned with marquetry inlaid carvings and the walls were fitted with elaborately filigreed woods. Crystal chandeliers dangled overhead, brocaded draperies flanked the windows, and the floor was covered by an exquisite Oriental carpet. To the front of the car was a kitchen, complete with a retinue of two waiters and a chef. The larder was stuffed with champagne and wine and an exotic variety of gourmet foods. To the rear was a master bedroom, with a commodious featherbed and a private bath. French mirrors, ornate with gilt, were scattered throughout the car, and special attention had been devoted to the bedroom. The experience was not unlike sleeping in a hall of mirrors.

Today, however, Tallman's thoughts were not on creature comforts. With dusk rapidly settling over the Sierras, he puffed on his cigar and pondered the vagaries of his profession. He found a certain irony in his latest assignment.

Some philosopher had once noted that every great fortune starts with a crime. Tallman thought the remark particularly apt when applied to the Southern Pacific Railroad. Along with its sister company, the Central Pacific, the railway line was controlled by a coalition known as the Big Four. In addition to Leland Stanford, president of the line, there were three partners: Charles Crocker, Mark Hopkins and Collis Huntington. Absolute magicians with accounting ledgers, the four men had made their fortunes by defrauding both the public and the federal government. Estimates of their thievery ranged upwards of fifty million dollars.

Like all robber barons, the Big Four combined politics with business. While building their half of the transcontinental line—the Central Pacific—they were granted nine million acres in federal land and twenty-four million dollars in government bonds. Another seventy million dollars was raised in corporate bond issues and the sale of stock. A separate construction company was then created, with the Big Four as the sole stockholders. Stanford and his partners channeled all funds through the construction company, and completed the railroad at a cost of forty-four million dollars. The balance, split four ways, allowed each man to pocket in excess of twelve million. Yet their chicanery had only just begun.

Before long, the Southern Pacific was known as the "Octopus" of California. With graft and bribes, the Big Four gained control of the state house and the legislature and a veritable army of lesser politicians. Their immense power allowed them to absorb not only rival railroads but steamships and coal mines, and vast landholdings along the Pacific Slope. Not content to be robber barons, they set out to create a kingdom by the sea. In time, through a mix of political corruption and monopolistic business methods, their goal was realized. The Southern Pacific "Octopus" ruled California.

All the way from Chicago, Tallman had reflected on the curious alliance of the Big Four and Allan Pinkerton. He knew Pinkerton to be a man of scrupulous honesty and high morals. The agency chief loathed criminals with a sort of religious fervor, and he was an ardent critic of corruption in government. While ambitious, he was devoid of greed and the love of cold power. Yet, by some odd quirk of personality, he admired and openly courted both the robber barons and unsavory politicians. Over the years, he had aligned himself, and the agency, with industrial tycoons, bankers and railroad magnates, and a gaggle of power brokers within the political establishment. To a large extent, he had paradoxically made the Pinkerton Agency the tool of those he found most reprehensible.

For his own part, Tallman remained somewhat detached, almost an observer. He subscribed to no particular ideology, and he'd never felt compelled to take up the banner in the name of lost causes. In a world largely controlled by rascals, he accepted the fact that principle must sometimes be tempered with pragmatism. He was amused by the antics of the robber barons, and his attitude toward them was one of mild contempt. His personal philosophy revolved around a simple axiom. All men, including the high muckamucks of business and politics, would one day wind up worm pudding. The party stopped at the grave, and in the end, no man inherited more than six feet of earth. So he devoted himself to the here and now, with special emphasis on wine, women and song. For he thought it exceedingly likely that the hereafter would be a very dull place. He savored today and gave short odds on tomorrow.

"Penny for your thoughts."

The voice broke Tallman's spell. He turned from the window and found Vivian standing beside his chair. She was freshly bathed and gave off a sensual radiation as palpable as musk. Her dress was teal blue, and in the last rays of sunset, she was a vision of loveliness. Tallman wagged his head and grinned.

"Try a dime a dozen and you might get your money's worth."

"Thanks a lot." Vivian gave him a pouty look and settled

into a nearby chair. "You could have lied a little and said you were mooning over me."

"No need to lie," Tallman mugged, hands outstretched. "You already know I'm yours to command."

"Won't that be the day." Vivian looked at him with impudent eyes. "No secrets between partners . . . remember?"

Tallman took a long draw on his cigar. "In the simplest possible terms . . . I was thinking we've been hired by a batch of crooks to put the quietus on a pack of hooligans."

"Well, shut my mouth!" Vivian's eyes got wide and round. "Once you unload, you do call a spade a spade, don't you?"

"The only difference between the Southern Pacific and the Settler's League is that our employers, wise men that they are, have the law on their side."

"And we're the hired mercenaries—correct?"

"You'll earn your detective's badge yet." Tallman watched her with an indulgent smile.

Vivian was a spitfire of a woman, and uniquely desirable. She was statuesque, with magnificent breasts, a tiny waist and long, lissome legs. She had extraordinary green eyes, exquisite features, and a cloud of auburn hair worn in the upswept fashion. She carried herself erect and proud, and when she smiled it was like sunrise on autumn leaves, somehow warm and sultry. She was bright and articulate, and as mentally acute as a faro dealer. Moreover, she was a woman of good-humored irony, and possessed a bawdy wit that saw the world in its proper perspective. He thought she was made-to-order for the detective business.

Over the past month, while her training was underway, they had entered into a torrid sexual liaison. He'd always thought his own approach to lovemaking uninhibited, without strictures or taboos. Yet he'd found in Vivian a creature of wild and explosive passion. She gloried in her sexuality, and her tastes ran the gamut from bizarre to outrageous. She was a woman who loved to make love, tempestuous and hot-blooded, a student of erotica. For her, nothing carnal was beyond experiment or invention. And for him, she was a never-ending source of delight. He sometimes thought he'd met his match.

A short while after sundown, dinner was announced. With the waiters in attendance, Tallman and Vivian were seated at a candlelit table. Before them was a glittering array of silver and crystal and bone-white china, all meticulously arranged on a fine linen tablecloth. Wine was served with each course, and the chef sent out turtle soup, followed by a savory court bouillon and roast squab basted with honey. The *pièce de résistance* was a dark brown *daube glacée*. After fruit and cheese, coffee was served in delicate demitasse cups. Then, cradled in a silver ice bucket, a bottle of vintage champagne was brought to the table.

Tallman complimented the chef on his artistry, and dismissed the staff for the night. Soon the clattering in the kitchen ceased, and the men made their way to a Pullman car up forward. Once they were gone, Tallman locked the door to the private car and returned to the table. He broke out a fresh panatela and lit up in a wreath of smoke. Across the table, Vivian watched him with the languorous smile of one surfeited by rich food and heady wines. He raised his glass in a toast.

"Here's to the life of the gentry."

"I'll second that." Vivian sipped, then hoisted her glass higher. "A girl travels in style when she travels with Ash Tallman."

"I assure you, the pleasure's all mine."

"I don't believe a word of it," Vivian said brightly. "But you're a sweetheart to say so."

"Are you questioning my word? The word of a gentleman and a scholar—and a Pinkerton dick!"

"Ummm!" Vivian leaned forward and her low-cut gown dipped lower. "You've just said the magic word!"

"Careful Viv!" Tallman stared at the vee of her breasts. "You're about to spill out of that dress."

Vivian moistened her lower lip and a vixen look touched her eyes. "Why don't you help me?"

"Help you what?"

"Help me"—she vamped him with a warm beguiling grin—"out of my dress, of course."

Tallman cocked one ribald eye at her and rose from his chair. She uttered a low, gloating laugh and stood as he moved around the table. He held out his arms and she stepped into his embrace. Her hands went behind his neck, pulling his head down, and she kissed him with a fierce, passionate urgency. Her mouth opened and his tongue performed deep, sensual probes. Then his arms tightened, strong and demanding, and she felt his cock harden against her thigh. When at last they parted, her voice was warm and husky.

"I want you, Ash. I want you now."

Tallman swept her off her feet and effortlessly lifted her in his arms. Her eyes gleamed with pleasure and her musical laughter was like wind chimes in a zephyr breeze.

Her tongue darted into his ear and a slow, dark smile played across his features as he buried his face in her breasts. She shuddered convulsively, squirming and peppering him with kisses, and their eyes locked in a moment of fiery anticipation. Then he gave her a jolly wink and carried her toward the rear of the car.

The mirrored walls in the bedroom shimmered with the umber glow of lamplight. He lowered her gently to the floor and they silently watched one another undress. Within moments they were naked and she stood before him with sculptured legs and high full breasts, her body rounded and youthful. She snuggled close in his arms, feeling an almost unbearable excitement as his hand teased her nipples erect. She eagerly sought his mouth, then her hand grasped his cock and she seated herself on the edge of the bed. She held his manhood in both hands, fondled it lovingly, and slowly stroked the underside with the tip of her tongue. He groaned as she took the head into her mouth.

Watching her in the mirrors, he took her head in his hands and guided her back and forth. Her mouth was slippery and wet, and as she sucked on him her tongue moved in quick little circles. She cupped his balls in her hands, caressed them tenderly, and felt them expand into throbbing stones. His cock was rigid and swollen, and she went down on it, swallowing the whole of him. Her head bobbed faster, up and down, with her tongue wet against the rigid length of his shaft. His back suddenly arched and his hands stopped her with a viselike grip.

"Blow it or fuck it—your choice!"

Vivian held him deep in her throat a moment and then

let go. She sprawled backwards on the bed and spread her legs wide. He bent down and his hand went to the curly delta between her thighs. His fingers found her vulva and he massaged the tiny rosebud skillfully. She was ready for him, moist and yielding, her damp muff an abundant swell of flesh. He lowered himself onto her and their mouths met in a feverish rush. His cock penetrated quickly and rammed to the hot, wet core.

A moan escaped her throat and she drove at him in an agonized clash, legs wrapped around his back. His arms went beneath her as he pressed closer still, until her buttocks clove tight to his loins. His stroke quickened, thrusting faster and deeper. Her body was wracked by explosive shudders, and she bucked to meet him, hips moving in frenzied circles. Then he drove his cock violently into her and exploded, his hot jolting eruptions carrying her across the threshold. Her nails clawed his back and she clung to him, screaming as wave after wave of orgasm engulfed her.

THREE

The muzzy fog slowly retreated before a bright morning sun. The hills of San Francisco stood sentinel over the curving shore of the bay. There, mast upon mast, vessels from around the world rode at anchor. To the west, the Golden Gate strait was still shrouded in mist.

Somewhat south of the city, the Southern Pacific railroad yards were located not far from the wharves. A short distance away locomotives huffed and hissed as passenger trains routinely departed the depot. In the yard itself, with several engines constantly in service, the dull whump of freight cars being coupled was not unlike a cannonade. The private car, shunted onto a nearby siding, sat alone amidst the commotion.

Knotting his tie, Tallman watched through the bedroom window. Late the night before the westbound express had arrived in San Francisco and the private car had been uncoupled without delay. Only minutes afterwards a messenger had appeared with a terse note from Otis Blackburn. Obviously a man of few words, the line's general superintendent had made no reference to the forthcoming investigation. He had simply informed Tallman to expect him at ten in the morning. The note had been signed with the precise penmanship of a bookkeeper.

Now, scarcely five minutes before the hour, Tallman finished dressing with no apparent haste. He shrugged into a shoulder holster rig and cinched the bottom of the holster to his belt with a leather thong. Crafted by hand, the holster had been wet-molded to a Colt New Line revolver. The front side of the holster was open and the revolver was retained by clip-springs sewn into the leather. The rig was fashioned for concealment and speed, designed to hug the body while affording instant access. A quick pull popped the gun through the springs and into the firing position.

Tallman's choice of weapons was dictated by the nature of his work. When operating undercover, it was generally wiser to appear unarmed. The Colt New Line was a stubby five-shot revolver chambered for .41 caliber. The barrel length was three and a half inches and the sheathed trigger was activated by cocking the hammer. Tallman also carried a hideout gun in a spring-loaded sleeve holster. Strapped to his right wrist, muzzle forward, was a Remington derringer, which was chambered for .41 caliber and held two rounds. By pressing his forearm to his side, the spring mechanism was released and snapped the gun forward into his hand. All one motion, the maneuver was literally quicker than the eye.

Speed alone, however, was not Tallman's primary concern. When gunplay proved necessary, his one goal was to stop an opponent on the spot. Over a period of time he had worked with a master gunsmith in developing explosive-tipped cartridges. The end product was a fiendish device, employing the basic laws of physics. A hole was drilled into the base of the bullet and a drop of quicksilver was then inserted into the cavity. After the base of the slug was resealed, it was loaded into a standard cartridge casing. Upon being fired, the forward momentum flattened the quicksilver against the rear of the cavity. Upon impact, however, the slug was slowed by the resistance of muscle and flesh and the heavy drop of quicksilver continued onward at the original velocity of the bullet. The collision of quicksilver and lead exploded the slug outward like a firecracker bursting apart.

The effect was devastating. When struck by an explosive bullet, a man's innards were literally blown to smithereens. Death was almost instantaneous, and one shot generally stopped the fight immediately. For good reason, then, Tallman loaded the Remington derringer with explosive-tipped cartridges. Vivian also carried a concealed derringer, and it too was loaded with exploding bullets. She readily adhered to Tallman's philosophy regarding kill-or-get-killed shootouts. Survival was the only thing that counted, and there were no second place winners. So it was better to do the killing swiftly and in the most expedient fashion possible. Explosive slugs eliminated the chance of error.

Tallman inspected himself in the mirror. His suit jacket fitted perfectly, and there were no telltale bulges to betray either the shoulder holster or the sleeve rig. Satisfied, he walked from the bedroom and moved forward through the car. Vivian was seated in one of the armchairs, buffing her nails. She wore a pleated skirt with a high-necked blouse, and her hair shone radiantly in the sunlight. She glanced around as Tallman approached and halted beside her chair.

"All ready to meet the big nabob?" she asked.

"I doubt that Blackburn qualifies for the title. People like Leland Stanford rarely soil their hands with the dirty work. That's left to an intermediary—a go-between."

"In other words, a glorified messenger boy."

"For the most part," Tallman affirmed. "Whatever Blackburn says will be exactly what Stanford told him to say. No more, no less."

A knock sounded at the door and Vivian smiled. "Well, he's prompt anyway."

"Behave yourself," Tallman admonished her. "Act demure and ladylike, and let me do the talking."

"Demure!" Vivian's eyes sparkled mischievously. "I lost that quality years ago, along with my virginity."

One of the waiters rushed to open the door. Otis Blackburn stepped inside and strode importantly through the car. He was short and stocky, with a stiff bearing and an abrasive expression. He looked like a querulous child sent to perform an unpleasant errand. His gaze touched on Vivian as he removed his hat and stopped. Then his attention shifted to Tallman.

"Otis Blackburn," he said with a perfunctory handshake. "I take it you're Ash Tallman?"

"At your service." Tallman let go of his hand and turned slightly. "Allow me to introduce Miss Vivian Valentine."

Blackburn examined her with a beady stare. "I understood you were being accompanied by another operative."

"Miss Valentine," Tallman said evenly, "is one of our top undercover agents."

"A woman?" Blackburn arched one eyebrow and looked down his nose. "I never heard of a female Pinkerton."

"Nor have most people," Tallman reported succinctly. "Which makes Miss Valentine doubly valuable in the field. She's our best kept secret."

"It won't do," Blackburn said shortly. "The job's too dangerous for a woman."

"Looks are deceiving," Vivian interrupted with a devilish smile. "I'm really a very dangerous lady, Mr. Blackburn."

"Maybe you are," Blackburn said, a note of irritation in his tone. "But that's neither here nor there. We requested Tallman and another operative—a male operative!"

"Quite understandable," Tallman interjected smoothly. "However, Allan Pinkerton permits me to choose my own partners. I assure you he trusts my judgment in such matters."

Blackburn looked annoyed. "You don't seem to get the point. In *my* judgment, a woman isn't suitable. And I speak for the Southern Pacific Railway."

"Then I suggest you wire Pinkerton and request another team."

"What's that?" Blackburn screwed up his face in a tight knot. "Are you refusing the assignment?"

"No," Tallman said simply. "I'm merely saying I either work with Miss Valentine or I don't work."

"Preposterous!" Blackburn fixed him with a baleful look. "How dare you try to bullyrag me!"

Tallman's genial features toughened. "All I've done is offer you an option—take it or leave it."

"Are you in the habit of dictating terms to a client?"

"Not terms," Tallman said quietly. "Let's call it a condition. You take me, then you take my partner too. And at the moment, that happens to be Miss Valentine."

There was a long pause of weighing and appraisal while the two men examined one another. A pained expression fell over Blackburn's face and his jaws worked as though he was grinding his teeth. At last, he took a deep breath and released it slowly.

"Very well," he said with a kind of smothered wrath. "Your condition is accepted. But I want it understood that you—and you alone—will be held accountable in the event anything goes wrong."

"I'm always accountable." Tallman motioned with an idle gesture. "Have a chair, Mr. Blackburn. I believe you planned to brief us on the case. Suppose we get to it?"

Blackburn seated himself opposite Vivian. She exchanged a quick glance with Tallman and he gave her a hidden wink. Then he lowered himself into a chair and turned his gaze on Blackburn. The silence thickened.

"The situation," Blackburn said at length, "involves an organized conspiracy whose aim is to defraud the Southern Pacific Railroad."

Tallman stopped him with an upraised palm. "We're already aware of the squatter problem and the Settlers' League. Your letter to Pinkerton was fairly clear on that score. What we need are specifics about the alleged conspiracy."

"Alleged?" Blackburn repeated churlishly. "Wrecked trains and blown bridges aren't alleged. Those are cold, hard facts."

"Hard facts and hard evidence aren't necessarily one and

the same. To build a case—even to start our investigation—we need specific details."

"Such as?"

"Who are the leaders of the Settlers' League?"

"Insofar as we can determine, it's controlled by one man. His name is Major Thomas McQuade. I understand he's a former army officer."

"Was he responsible for organizing the League?"

"I have no idea," Blackburn said solemnly. "He's a squatter himself, and he's been the guiding force behind the League's legal efforts. So we can assume he's also the ringleader behind the conspiracy."

"I never assume anything," Tallman said with a measured smile. "Exactly how many squatters are there?"

"Forty-three," Blackburn said crisply. "By that I mean there are forty-three families, each occupying a quarter-section of land."

"According to your letter, the land in question is located in the San Joaquin Valley."

"That's correct."

Blackburn pulled a small map from his inside jacket pocket. He unfolded it and spread it between them. Marks indicating railroad tracks bisected the state, from San Francisco to Los Angeles. His finger traced a southerly route to Fresno, then skipped lower to the town of Hanford. Located halfway down the map, the town was on the eastern edge of the San Joaquin Valley. Somewhat farther east lay the Sierra Nevada Range.

"The Settlers' League," Blackburn said, tapping the map, "has its headquarters in Hanford. All the squatters occupy land along our right of way north and south of town."

Tallman mulled it over a minute. "How did they gain control of the land?"

"By squatting on it," Blackburn said indignantly. "So far, our legal efforts haven't budged them an inch."

"Are there squatters in other areas besides Hanford?"

"Not yet," Blackburn responded. "We were lax and allowed things to go too far in Hanford. Now we want it stopped before it spreads."

Tallman studied him for a long, speculative moment, "Our instructions were to infiltrate the League and gather evidence of a criminal conspiracy. I get the impression you're suggesting something more."

"I am indeed," Blackburn said crisply. "Once you have the necessary proof, we will then take the initiative. Our plans are to arrange an incident which will force Major McQuade and his League into an open confrontation."

"What sort of confrontation?"

"A couple of our men will proceed to Hanford and physically evict one of the squatter families. We can reasonably expect that McQuade and his people will resort to violence in an effort to reoccupy the farm. At that point, our chances of securing a conspiracy indictment will be greatly enhanced."

"Aren't you concerned about the safety of your men? By provoking violence, you might easily get them killed."

"Not these boys!" Blackburn blustered. "They can handle themselves. . . ."

Tallman's face took on a sudden hard cast. "You're talking about professional gunmen."

"The best money can buy," Blackburn chortled.

"Besides, we own the sheriff in Kings County. So it's all cut and dried from start to finish."

"I see," Tallman said tightly. "What you've just outlined exceeds my instructions. In fact, the plan itself borders on conspiracy. I'll have to check with Allan Pinkerton before we proceed further."

Blackburn's eyes suddenly turned angry, commanding. "You are in the employ of the Southern Pacific. Leland Stanford issues the orders here and you will follow them to the letter."

"Then trot Stanford down here and let me hear the orders direct."

"Mr. Stanford doesn't deal with detectives. You will report to me and me alone!"

"I report to Pinkerton and nobody else. He can keep Stanford advised . . . or not . . . as he chooses."

"I repeat," Blackburn said with a withering scowl, "you will take your orders from me and you will report to me."

Tallman gave him a satiric look. "See that mirror?"

Blackburn darted a glance at the wall mirror. "What about it?"

"Walk over there and kiss yourself good-bye."

"Don't get smart with me." Blackburn bristled. "You're hired help and this railroad car happens to be Southern Pacific property."

Tallman rose and jerked his thumb toward the door. "We'll let Pinkerton and Stanford decide who calls the shots."

"Try it and you're in for a rude awakening!"

"Perhaps." A strange light came into Tallman's eyes.

"Now, you'd better leave before I lose my temper and do something boorish."

Blackburn's face went black. He muttered an unintelligible oath and jackknifed to his feet. Then he turned with a kind of military abruptness and stumped out of the car. The door slammed shut with a jarring thud.

"Whew!" Vivian let out her breath. "You sure know how to butter up a client."

"Listen and learn," Tallman observed wryly. "What happens when Pinkerton and Stanford exchange telegrams?"

"Blackburn will run to Stanford," Vivian said with a look of revelation. "Stanford will wire Pinkerton, then Pinkerton will wire you. And you'll have your orders in writing!"

Tallman's grin was so wide it was almost a laugh. "I think you just earned your detective's badge."

FOUR

The San Joaquin Valley shimmered beneath a blazing sun. The afternoon sky boiled with clouds drifting westward and the green earth steamed with heat. Huffing smoke and fiery cinders, the train followed a meandering course southward.

Tallman was seated beside an open window. The interior of the passenger coach was like a blast furnace, and the warm air rushing through the window did little to relieve his discomfort. His shirt was plastered to his skin and a film of sweat glistened on his forehead. Yet the revolver underneath his arm, and the derringer strapped to his wrist, made it impossible for him to remove his coat. He endured, and stared listlessly out at the countryside.

To the west, the Coastal Range screened the ocean from view. Eastward, some thirty miles distant, the towering spires of the Sierra Nevada Range jutted skyward. From there, the waters of several tributaries flowed into the central basin of the San Joaquin Valley. The Kings River, which paralleled the railroad tracks, was one such stream. Snow melt-off coursed downward from the mountains throughout the spring and early summer, and provided a natural irrigation system the year round. The end product was a land lush with vegetation and boundless graze.

Wearied with the scenery, Tallman's thoughts were on Vivian and the next step in their assignment. Hardly to his surprise, he'd received a telegram late yesterday from Allan Pinkerton. The message was concise and bluntly stated: He was to consider any order from Otis Blackburn a direct order from Leland Stanford, and conduct himself accordingly. After the telegram, and another session with Blackburn, Tallman had played the good soldier. The plan hatched in the offices of the Southern Pacific would be followed to the letter.

The field operation was an altogether different matter. Tallman brooked interference from no one with regard to an undercover investigation. Once more Blackburn had been shown the door, and told to await developments. The balance of the evening, with Vivian a rapt listener, Tallman had worked out his own approach to the assignment. It bore his usual mark of chicanery and craft.

After a final night with Vivian, Tallman had boarded the morning southbound. His destination was Hanford, where he personally planned to infiltrate the Settlers' League. His cover story, though a complete fabrication, was both plausible and convincing. Vivian was to follow him by a day, and establish herself in Fresno. Located just north of the Kings County line, Fresno was the major trade center of the eastern basin. Once there, Vivian was to pose as a vagabond saloon girl and obtain employment in one of the town's dives. By keeping her ears open, she was certain to uncover the latest gossip about the squatters' vendetta with the Southern Pacific. When the time seemed opportune, Tallman would contact her directly. Until then she was to take no action on her own.

Late that afternoon, with the sun retreating slowly westward, the train pulled into Hanford. Tallman collected his luggage and emerged from the coach onto the depot platform. He walked to the end of the station house, rounding the corner, and then stopped. Ahead lay the town's main thoroughfare, with the business district stretching some three blocks upstreet. He dropped his bag and lit a cigar, scrutinizing the scene with a look of mild wonder. Hanford was something more than he'd expected.

The town was a tableau of thriving commerce. Shops and business establishments were ranked along a dusty street wide enough to accommodate three wagons abreast. On one side was a livery stable and a saloon, bank and billiard hall, hardware store and hotel. On the opposite side was a blacksmith and a butcher shop, newspaper and general emporium, pharmacy and restaurant. In addition, wedged in among the other buildings, were a barber shop, doctor's office and a large grocery store. The boardwalks were crowded with people and farm wagons lined the street. The county courthouse, which dominated the far end of town, was flanked by a church and a schoolhouse of modest proportions. A residential area fanned outward from the downtown district with homes bracketed by whitewashed picket fences. Hanford looked as though it had been built to last.

Hefting his bag, Tallman walked up the street. He was somehow bothered by the look of permanence and bustling trade. From his talks with Otis Blackburn, he'd formed the impression that Hanford was a jerkwater burg on the fringe of nowhere. Instead, he'd found a prosperous community laid out with an eye to the future. Quite obviously, the town fathers had organized Hanford with visions of growth and the promise of expanding agriculture throughout the countryside. None of which gibed with illegal squatters and a Settlers' League pitted in a do-or-die fight against the railroad. All in all, the situation appeared to merit closer investigation. Hanford looked like anything but a hotbed of anarchists.

Tallman proceeded directly to the hotel. He entered the lobby and crossed to the registration desk. The clerk was a rumpled man, balding and potbellied, with wire-rimmed glasses perched on the tip of his nose. He rose from a battered rolltop desk and moved to the counter. He gave Tallman a slow once-over, noting the spiffy attire and the leather suitcase. He nodded with bored affability.

"Afternoon."

"Good afternoon," Tallman said breezily. "I want to engage your best room. Preferably one with a private bath and a good view."

"I take it you're a city feller?"

"Oh?" Tallman played along. "Why so?"

"Otherwise you wouldn't ask for a private bath. There's no such animal in this neck of the woods."

"A pity," Tallman murmured. "Well, then, perhaps a room close to the lavatory."

"No problem there," the clerk crackled. "Washstand in your room and a johnny-pot under the bed. We empty it twice a day, regular as clockwork."

"What more could a man ask? I'll take it."

"How long will you be stayin'?"

"Now, there's the question," Tallman said pleasantly. "Perhaps you could be of some service—a matter of information."

"Try me and see."

"Alex Fitzhugh," Tallman stuck out his hand. "Attorney at law."

"A lawyer, huh?" The clerk accepted his handshake. "I'm Bob Simpson. I own the joint, all twelve rooms."

"Capital!" Tallman beamed. "An entrepreneur and businessman. Doubtless you know everything there is to know about Hanford."

"Maybe," Simpson allowed. "You here to take somebody to court?"

"Indeed not," Tallman boomed out jovially. "I'm considering establishing my law practice in your fair city."

"No shit?" Simpson appeared bemused. "Whatever gave you a notion like that?"

"Well, for one thing, Hanford is the county seat. For another, I've been told there's a scarcity of lawyers in these parts."

"You was told right," Simpson acknowledged. "Not that our courthouse ain't a pretty lively place. But most lawyers figger they can get here quick enough when duty calls. The ones I know operate out of Fresno."

"Excellent!" Tallman's smile broadened. "A burgeoning metropolis like Hanford needs a resident attorney. I do believe I'll spend a few days exploring the potential."

"You could do lots worse, I suppose."

"My very thought, Mr. Simpson."

Tallman signed the register with a flourish. Simpson

insisted on carrying his bag and showed him to an up-stairs room with a view of Main Street. A gadfly of sorts, Simpson volunteered a wealth of information about Hanford and its leading citizens. He dwelt at length on the Settlers' League and the Southern Pacific, which provided unending fodder for the town's gossipmill. Tallman expressed a lawyerly interest, but held his questions to a general nature. In response to questions about himself, he paraded out a cover story that involved a law practice back East, followed by a ruinous divorce and the search for a fresh start out West. The hotel owner finally departed with the look of a cat spitting feathers.

For his part, Tallman was inwardly delighted with the exchange. Simpson was a marathon talker and no great believer in keeping what he knew to himself. By nightfall, word of the newly arrived lawyer would have spread throughout town. Which was precisely what Tallman had intended the moment he'd stepped off the train. In the guise of Alex Fitzhugh, he would scarcely be a stranger to anyone who counted in Hanford.

Things were cooking along even better than he'd expected.

Darkness had fallen when Tallman emerged from the hotel. Streetlamps flickered like clusters of candles along the street, and the business district was virtually deserted. Hanford's lone restaurant was a couple of blocks down and he walked in that direction. Then, on the spur of the moment, he decided to stop off at the saloon. A sociable drink would further establish his presence in town.

The crowd inside the saloon was a mixed bag of tricks. Townsmen and farmers were bellied up to the bar, talking in low monotones. A couple of drummers, distinguishable by their flashy suits and bowler hats, were seated at a table. Several other men, with the look of prosperity and position, occupied a table toward the rear. All heads turned as Tallman came through the door and approached the bar. There was a momentary lull while everyone in the room subjected him to quick examination. Then the buzz of conversation once more resumed.

Tallman took a spot at the end of the bar. He ordered rye whiskey and paid when the barkeep filled his glass. After a long sip, he hooked his foot over the brass rail and fished a panatela from inside his suit jacket. He lit the cigar, puffing wads of smoke, all the while aware he was being observed by those nearby. Wary of moving too fast too quickly, he decided to make no overtures himself. Sooner or later one of the locals would succumb to curiosity and strike up a conversation. Until then, it was best to mind saloon etiquette and not butt in unless invited. He sipped his rye and pretended to be immersed in his own thoughts.

On the third sip, the farmer standing beside him abruptly pushed away from the bar. The movement jostled Tallman's arm and rye sloshed out of his glass onto the counter. The farmer whirled on him with a bulldog scowl.

"Watch who you're shovin'!"

The room went still and Tallman sensed an undercurrent of tension. The farmer was a bruiser, heavily muscled, with a thick neck and powerful shoulders. He reeked of whiskey and manure, and his eyes were bloodshot with drink. He glowered at Tallman with a look of animal ferocity.

"No harm done," Tallman said agreeably. "Let me buy you a drink."

"In a pig's ass! Nobody shoves me and gets away with it!"

"I assure you, I intended no offense."

"Slick talker, ain't you?" The farmer spat on his hands and rubbed them together. "Put up your dukes, sonnyboy. I'm gonna stunt your growth!"

Tallman grinned ruefully. "You're absolutely certain there's no other way?"

"Gawddamn certain!"

The farmer launched a looping haymaker. Tallman sidestepped, landing a quick jab followed by a whistling left hook. Unfazed, the farmer snarled a murderous oath and threw a clubbing roundhouse. Slipping the blow, Tallman bobbed inside and buried his fist in the farmer's underbelly. The farmer's mouth popped open and he clutched his groin in agony. Tallman set himself and exploded a splintering combination, a left hook and a thunderbolt right cross. The farmer went down like a wet bag of sand. His head struck the brass rail and his jaws snapped shut with an audible click. He was out cold.

A leaden silence enveloped the saloon. No one moved and all eyes were trained on Tallman with open amazement. Then, suddenly, one of the men at the rear table rose and walked forward. He was corded and lean, with a neatly trimmed beard and stern features. His whole bearing was charged with energy and he moved through the crowd with a commanding presence. He was attired in a somber frock coat and his overall appearance was one of prosperity and substance. Yet, upon closer inspection, there was a strangeness about him. His eyes were dull and marble-like, curiously without life or expression. He halted in front of Tallman.

"Allow me to apologize, Mr. Fitzhugh." He gestured at the fallen farmer. "Floyd Hull's a hothead who can't handle his liquor. You gave him no more than he deserved."

"No apology necessary, Mr.—"

"Major Thomas McQuade." He extended his hand in a firm grasp. "You'll have to excuse our small-town ways. Bob Simpson, who owns the hotel, hasn't stopped wagging his tongue since you arrived."

"McQuade?" Tallman paused with a quizzical look. "Of course, I remember now. Simpson mentioned that you're chairman of the Settlers' League. I was most impressed by your legal dispute with the railroad."

"Quite natural, considering your profession. I understand you're a lawyer?"

"Without a practice, I fear." Tallman opened his hands and shrugged. "I'm looking for a place to hang my shingle."

"So I heard," McQuade said. "According to Simpson, you've just come West. May I ask how you happened to pick Hanford? We're somewhat off the beaten track."

"Process of elimination," Tallman lied heartily. "I stopped off at Sacramento and checked the Bar Association records. I was looking for a town without a lawyer, and Hanford appeared the most promising of the lot. So here I am."

"Well, if your pugilistic skills are any indication, you must be a holy terror in the courtroom. How did a lawyer get so handy with his fists?"

"Princeton," Tallman said with a lopsided grin. "Class of '69. I won the collegiate heavyweight championship—three years running."

"After tonight, no one will argue the point. You've certainly made your mark in Hanford, Mr. Fitzhugh. I wouldn't doubt that folks will welcome a lawyer with your combative style."

"All I need now is a client."

McQuade studied him with deliberate appraisal. "How good are you in a courtroom?"

"Better than most," Tallman said with cocky pride. "Why, are you in need of legal advice?"

"Perhaps," McQuade said tentatively. "What do you know about our fight with the Southern Pacific?"

"Very little." Tallman's expression betrayed nothing. "Bob Simpson told me your case has been appealed to the Supreme Court. But he was rather vague on details."

"Small wonder," McQuade growled. "Our own lawyer hasn't been able to make heads nor tails of the decision."

"Who represented you?"

"Ambrose Sloan," McQuade said with a frown. "He has offices in Fresno. So far as we're concerned, he lost an unlosable case. We held all the cards."

"Sounds interesting."

McQuade eyed him keenly. "It occurs to me that you might be Johnny-on-the-spot, Mr. Fitzhugh. We could damn sure use a second opinion."

"Needless to say"—Tallman smiled crookedly—"I'm available. Of course, I would have to review the particulars. From what I've heard thus far, it's a case of some complexity."

"Amen to that." McQuade hesitated, thoughtful for a time. "Tell you what, Alex. You don't mind me calling you Alex, do you?"

"By no means."

"Good," McQuade nodded briskly. "Folks around here generally call me Major."

"A privilege and an honor—Major."

"Well, anyway," McQuade went on, "I started to say we're having a League meeting tomorrow night. Why don't you plan on attending and I'll introduce you to the members. I've no doubt they'll go along with the idea."

Floyd Hull groaned and rolled onto his side. He retched, coughing raggedly, and spit out a bloody molar. McQuade glanced down with a look of distaste and slowly shook his head. Then he turned smartly on his heel. "Come on, Alex. I'll buy you a drink and we'll hash out some of those particulars you mentioned."

Tallman dutifully trailed along. He suppressed a wild urge to laugh out loud; instead, he silently congratulated himself on a nifty piece of work. He'd played into luck and improvised as the situation unfolded. The upshot was that he'd gaffed a prize sucker fish. And if his information was correct, the next step would be simpler yet.

FIVE

Vivian's hotel room was bleaker than a nun's cell. The mattress on the bed sagged in the middle and the bed linen itself was dingy with age. The pitcher on the washstand was cracked and the wall mirror was faded to a ghostly blur. The sole stick of furniture was a rickety straightbacked chair.

Stripped to her undergarments, Vivian stood peering into the mirror. She slowly colored her cheeks with a garish magenta shade of rouge. Next she darkened her eyelids with kohl, spreading it high and wide until the greenfire of her eyes seemed to blaze like emeralds set in dusky onyx. Then she dabbed her lips dry and methodically set about painting them into a vermilion beestung pucker.

While she worked, Vivian mentally reviewed her role in the undercover operation. Her assignment, as outlined by Ash Tallman, was to pose as a down-on-her-luck saloon girl. Accordingly, she had spent yesterday scouring San Francisco for the paraphernalia necessary to her disguise. Late last evening, she had boarded the overnight southbound, carrying a carpetbag stuffed with clothes purchased at a second-hand store. Shortly before noon, she had de-trained at Fresno and inquired directions to the sporting district. There she had selected a sleazy fleabag of a hotel and signed the register as Sally Randolph. Acting stony broke, she had taken a room for only one night. The desk clerk had been left with the impression that she was down to nickels and dimes.

Thus far, Vivian found undercover work not all that different from a con game. The idea was to establish a phony identity and a plausible cover story, and thereafter assume all the little quirks of character that made the performance believable. During her month in Chicago, Tallman had discovered that her experience as a bunco artist enabled her to act a part with consummate skill. The balance of her training had been devoted to the art of subtle interrogation; she learned all the tricks and devices of extracting information without arousing suspicion. She had learned as well that Tallman was unlike any of her previous lovers. A look, even a casual touch, was enough to leave her knees weak and a wet sensation between her legs. She wanted him inside her all the time, and her dreams were filled with visions of his phallus standing stiff and erect.

A realist, Vivian understood that Ash Tallman would never limit himself to one woman. He was no more monogamous than a bull in rutting season; women found him charming and irresistible, and it was his nature to play the field. Yet, while Vivian understood all that, the month in Chicago had nonetheless left her under his spell. For the first time in her life, she was jealous and possessive, and fairly burned with envy at the thought of his touching another woman. At the same time, she was reconciled to the fact that it would happen.

Once out of her sight, she knew he would dip into the first set of drawers that sparked his interest. So she warned herself to curb her feelings and accept the inevitable. She was also honest enough to admit that she wasn't exactly enthralled with the straight and narrow herself. She liked men and the idea of playing around still had a certain appeal. She was no alleycat, but she too had needs, and out of sight out of mind worked both ways. A fling here and there might very well do her a world of good. And since he was no celibate, her own diddling would simply even the score.

Today, though, Vivian's thoughts were on the job at hand. Her makeup complete, she inspected herself critically in the mirror. She looked brazen and tough, slightly vulgar, and yet compellingly attractive in a bawdy sort of way. Satisfied, she doused herself with cheap perfume and turned to her carpetbag. The dress she took out was wine colored and cut so skimpy it left little to the imagination. When she stepped into it, her breasts rose like melons out of the low-cut bodice and her tiny waist accentuated the round swell of her hips. She preened, watching herself in the mirror, and a vulpine smile appeared at the corner of her mouth. She had no doubt it would work like catnip on the sporting crowd.

With the derringer in her purse, she sailed out of the room and made her way downstairs. The desk clerk practically swallowed his teeth when he got a look at her tartish outfit. To her questions, his stuttered answers were delivered with an expression of pop-eyed lust. All of which convinced her that the overhaul job had indeed produced the desired effect. Five minutes later she walked from the hotel with the name of the town's swankiest dive and some small insight into the proprietor's taste in women. Outside, swinging her hips, she strolled off down Broadway.

Fresno was a hub of trade and commerce. Located in the heart of the San Joaquin Valley, it had something of a boomtown atmosphere. Its four banks underwrote crop loans to farmers and provided mortgage money for anyone with a deed to a quarter-section. Of still greater significance, the Southern Pacific had selected Fresno as its midway terminus in the state. The railroad's switching yards and warehouses were situated on the edge of town, and the sheer volume of traffic made it an around the clock operation. Not surprisingly, then, Fresno was the final marketplace for produce and livestock from throughout the central basin. Civic boosters touted it as the capital of the San Joaquin Valley.

The sporting district was an offshoot of Fresno's boomtown prosperity. Railroad men on layovers and farmers with money to burn were interested in diversion and entertainment. From the lower end of Broadway, several streets branched off to the outskirts of town. There, within a three-block radius, were to be found most of the gamier pursuits known to man. Saloons and dance halls, variety theaters and gambling dens all vied with one another for the nightly trade. Only one vice was missing within the town limits proper. The city council, drawing the line at the wages of sin, had exiled the kingdom of whores. County officials, however, displayed greater tolerance and a somewhat more receptive attitude toward bribes. A couple of feet across the town line was a collection of cribs and cathouses, staffed by ladies of negotiable virtue. The locals jestingly referred to it as Poonville.

A short walk from the hotel, Vivian turned off Broadway onto Elm. She proceeded halfway down the block and entered the Palace Variety Theater. The front end was a barroom and at the rear tables and chairs were clustered before a curtained stage. The interior was decorated in whorehouse red, with a large French mirror and several nude paintings lining the backbar wall. The establishment's chief attraction was a nightly card of burlesque acts, interspersed with a chorus line of buxom highsteppers. No cover charge was imposed on the clientele, but whiskey was a dollar a shot and loafers were unceremoniously treated to the bum's rush. The Palace catered to those who liked their entertainment and booze in equal parts.

A barkeep with a sweeping handlebar mustache pointed Vivian in the right direction. She went backstage and entered an office that was utilitarian by any standards. Apart from a desk and a chair, the furnishings consisted of a filing cabinet and a leather reclining sofa. The sofa was worn from use, and the man behind the desk looked like he used it most often when casting for chorus girls. He was thickset, almost brutish in appearance, with a bullet head and sagging jowls. His eyes were shifty and alert, and his expression was like that of a panting jackal. Vivian immediately tagged him as a horny old lech.

"Mr. Logan?" she simpered. "Mr. Horace Logan?"

"Yeah?"

"I'd like to talk with you . . . if you can spare a minute."

"Time's money," Logan said curtly. "What's on your mind?"

"I was told you run the classiest place in town."

"Who by?"

"The desk clerk at the Broadway Hotel."

"You must be on your uppers." Logan grunted sharply. "Nobody stays in that dump except streetwalkers and rumpots."

"I know," Vivian said with a theatrical shudder. "But a working girl can't always pick and choose. You know how it is, Mr. Logan."

"Lemme guess," Logan said stolidly. "Your money give out and you got yourself stranded in Fresno?"

"Well . . ." Vivian hesitated, her eyes downcast. "I could use a job, Mr. Logan. I thought maybe you'd have an opening."

"What's your specialty?"

"Uh—I dance a little and I carry a tune pretty good."

"Sing something."

"Beg pardon?"

"Go on." Logan waved a hand. "Lemme hear your voice. Show me a few dance steps."

"Tell you the truth," Vivian replied with a charming little shrug, "I can't carry a tune in a bucket. But you can't blame me for trying, Mr. Logan."

"So what do you do?"

"I'm a floor girl." Vivian graced him with a dazzling smile. "I hustle drinks like nobody you ever saw before."

Logan squinted at her. "I got all the girls I need. Why should I hire you?"

"Because I'm good." Vivian lifted her chin slightly. "I'll outhustle any two girls on the floor. You just try me and see!"

"Where've you worked before?"

"Frisco." Vivian's eyes were round and guileless. "I was one of the top girls on the Barbary Coast. Worked the last year at the Bella Union."

"That a fact?" Logan sounded impressed. "The Bella Union's a high-class joint. Why'd you leave?"

"Personal troubles." Vivian paused, met his gaze with an amused expression. "I got in too thick with a fellow and he wouldn't take no for an answer. So it was tie the knot or scram. I scrammed."

"You're not in dutch with the law, are you?"

Vivian threw back her head and laughed. "Not me. I'm on the up and up, Mr. Logan. Strictly legit."

"What's your name?"

"Sally Randolph."

Logan hooked his thumbs in his vest and examined her sumptuous figure. His eyes narrowed and a lewd smirk settled over his mouth. Vivian could scarcely mistake the nature of his look. Horace Logan was mentally undressing her and he obviously liked what he saw. The smirk widened into a smug grin.

"Close the door." He gestured to the reclining sofa. "Have a seat and we'll talk about it."

Vivian shook a roguish finger at him. "No monkey business, Mr. Logan. All I want is a job and a chance to prove myself."

Logan's grin turned oily. "All my girls put out before they get the job. It's a rule of the house."

"I'm not saying no"—Vivian's lips curved in a teasing smile—"but I'm not the screw-around type, Mr. Logan. I like to get to know a fellow first."

"Why should I make an exception?"

"Tell you what," Vivian bubbled. "Forget about paying me a salary. I'll work for half the bar tab I hustle and nothing else. What could be fairer than that?"

Logan gave her a jaundiced look. "No after-hours tricks. Whores aren't allowed inside the city limits, and I won't risk getting closed down. So don't try peddling pussy on the side, you understand?"

"I don't sell it," Vivian assured him earnestly. "I'd rather push drinks and pick my own bed partner."

"Speaking of which," Logan grumbled, "how long do I wait till you come across?"

"Not long." Vivian's voice was filled with promise. "I feel like I know you better already."

"You play me for a sucker and I'll fix it so you don't fuck nobody—ever again."

Vivian laughed an exhilarated laugh. "I always gave better blow jobs anyway."

Logan's mouth twisted in an ugly grin. "You just make sure you bob my apple first—got it?"

"Got it," Vivian said with a puckish smile. "When do I start work?"

"Tonight soon enough for you?"

"I'll be here."

Vivian left him to contemplate his rocklike hard-on. She figured a week at the most before he demanded payment on her promise. She thought it time enough to complete the assignment.

Shortly after the supper hour, men began streaming into the Palace. Soon it was three deep at the bar and more pushing through the door every minute. A bevy of girls circulated around the room, pausing here and there to hustle drinks. All heaving breasts and ruby-lipped smiles, they worked the crowd like sideshow carnies at top form.

Vivian was decked out in a peek-a-boo gown, bright with spangles. The dress was cut low on top and high on the bottom, and fashioned from hardly enough material to pad a crutch. Everything she had was enticingly displayed and drew appreciative stares as she drifted along the bar. Thus far, though she had concentrated on railroad men, she'd heard nothing of interest. Then, out of the corner of her eye, she saw a couple of uptown types enter the door. One was short and rotund, conservatively dressed. The other was thin and sleek, something of a dandy. She motioned to the nearest bartender.

"Who're the swells, over by the door?"

"The fat one's a banker, Benjamin Canby. His pal is a big shot lawyer, Ambrose Sloan."

"Just my speed." Vivian laughed. "I'm partial to the gentry."

A girl appeared at Vivian's elbow. She was busty and coarse, with a mop of blond, curly hair and freckles on her nose. She planted her hands on her hips.

"Steer clear!" she said with a feisty scowl. "Canby's mine and I don't like competition."

"Okay by me," Vivian told her. "I'll latch on to his chum."

"No soap," the girl said hotly. "Where one goes, the other goes. I've got 'em both staked out."

Vivian gave her a dirty look. "Why be greedy? We'll split the tab even-steven."

"I'm warning you—stay away or I'll scratch your goddamn eyes out!"

"C'mon, be a sport. Share the wealth."

"Kiss my ass and buzz off!"

Vivian laughed in her face. "You dumb bitch. Now listen close and pay attention." She lowered her voice to a vicious whisper. "You mess with me and I'll cut your tits off and stuff 'em up your nose. Get the idea?"

The girl's eyes veiled with caution. She suddenly looked slow and stupid and bewildered. After a moment, she turned and walked away with a faintly stricken expression. Vivian dismissed her without another thought and sauntered toward the front of the room. Approaching the two men, she stuck out her chest and seemed to jiggle all over. Then she gave them a brilliant smile.

"Mr. Canby, Mr. Sloan." She held out her arms. "I'm Sally Randolph. Welcome to the Palace!"

SIX

The Settlers' League meeting was scheduled for seven o'clock. As dusk cloaked the land, wagons began trundling into Hanford. The farmers arrived three or four to a wagon, unaccompanied by women or children. Tonight was not a social affair, evidenced by the fact that the men were armed with pistols and shotguns. All of them appeared somber and somehow troubled.

Major Thomas McQuade entered the hotel a few minutes before seven. The League meetings were held in a large room normally rented out for balls and other social occasions. Tallman rose from a chair as McQuade crossed the lobby. Over drinks the night before the Major had outlined the details of the League's protracted court battle. Tonight Tallman would be introduced to the members and allowed to attend a general planning session. McQuade would then put forth a motion that the League retain his services as a lawyer. It promised to be a busy and enlightening evening.

McQuade greeted him with a warm handshake. Standing off to one side, they conversed quietly as the farmers trooped through the lobby. A few of the men stopped by and McQuade performed introductions. The others merely nodded and proceeded on into the meeting room. The grapevine had worked overtime with word of the saloon brawl; by now, practically everyone in Kings County was aware that Floyd Hull had been soundly whipped in a dustup with the new lawyer. The general feeling was that Hull, who was something of a bully, had at last gotten his comeuppance. The incident had transformed Tallman into a celebrity of sorts, and the farmers inspected him with open curiosity as they walked past. He returned their stares with a look of genial interest.

"Good turnout," McQuade remarked. "Your little fracas last night apparently made the rounds. Everybody wants a gander at the man who licked Floyd Hull."

"Where is Hull?" Tallman inquired. "I thought he was a member of the League."

"Oh, he won't show." McQuade laughed. "You humiliated him, and he wouldn't make a public spectacle of himself tonight."

"No hard feelings on my part," Tallman said easily. "I'm willing to let bygones be bygones."

"I suspect Floyd wouldn't. He's been known to hold a grudge, and he never forgets a slight. You'd do well to watch yourself whenever he's around."

"You think he might want a rematch?"

"Not on the up and up," McQuade noted. "He'll bide his time and wait till you drop your guard. Then he'll jump you without warning and try to make quick work of it. I suggest you avoid allowing him any sort of edge."

"I'll keep my eyes open."

McQuade nodded and glanced past him. "On a more pleasant note, Angela Pryor just arrived. She's our recording secretary."

Tallman turned toward the door and registered a quick look of surprise. Somehow he'd expected an older woman, dowdy and careworn. Angela Pryor was a blond tawny cat of a girl, with bold hazel eyes and an impudent smile. While she was no orthodox beauty, her features were delicately structured and she seemed to radiate an aura of vivacity. Her ripe breasts and firm buttocks filled her gingham dress with spectacular effect, and she moved with uncommon grace for one so well endowed. All in all, she was a stunner.

"Very attractive," Tallman commented as she crossed the lobby. "Is her husband a member of the League?"

"No more," McQuade said softly. "She's a widow. Her man died last year and she took over the farm. Has to use hired help, but she's making a go of it."

"I wouldn't doubt it for a moment."

"Don't fool yourself," McQuade advised. "Angela doesn't trade on her looks. She's sharp as a tack."

"You'll get no argument there, Major."

Angela Pryor halted and McQuade introduced them. She fixed Tallman with a strange, inquisitive look and their eyes locked for an instant. Something unspoken passed between them, almost as though he were reading her mind. The message he got was part invitation and part challenge. He thought it quite likely her husband had died from overexertion, probably late at night. He moved his chin in an imperceptible nod.

"A pleasure to make your acquaintance, Mrs. Pryor."

"Thank you," Angela said with an animated smile. "I must say I've been looking forward to it myself. Anyone who beats the tar out of Floyd Hull is worth knowing."

Tallman brushed aside the compliment. "In the scheme of things, it was a rather minor event. The battle you folks are waging against the Southern Pacific seems to me a larger arena—and far more perilous."

"Spoken like a true gladiator. I do believe we've found ourselves an attorney equal to the task. Wouldn't you agree, Major McQuade?"

"All in good time," McQuade replied. "Suppose we get things underway and see where it leads? Then we'll let Mr. Fitzhugh decide for himself."

McQuade led the way into the meeting room. Chairs had been arranged in rows, and some forty men were already seated. Up front, three chairs had been placed behind a long wooden table. After Angela Pryor and Tallman were seated, McQuade moved to the center of the table. He rapped the tabletop sharply with his knuckles.

"Meeting will come to order!"

Conversation subsided and he stood for a moment gazing out at the farmers. Then he squared himself up in a lordly stance. "We're here to talk about the Octopus. You men are armed because the Southern Pacific is a law unto itself. None of us knows when we'll return home to find ourselves confronted by process servers and railroad thugs. I propose we set about changing that—tonight!"

A buzz of excitement swept through the crowd and McQuade quickly went on with his tirade. Tallman, though he appeared absorbed, actually listened with only half an ear. Some inner recess of his mind was separated, studying

the speaker rather than the words. Major Thomas Mc-
Quade was clearly accustomed to having his own way, and
it seemed unlikely he would be thwarted tonight. His attitude toward the farmers was one of amiable sufferance, the
hallmark of a firebrand skilled in the use of demagogy.
Any lingering doubt Tallman might have had was now
dispelled. The Settlers' League was the instrument of one
man, and none dared oppose him.

Tallman's preoccupation was suddenly broken. Mc-
Quade turned and leveled a finger directly at him. "Alex
Fitzhugh! He's new to town, but I don't need to tell you
boys he's a fighter. And by God that's what we need in our
corner—a fighter!"

There was a moment of stark silence. Then one of the
farmers meekly raised his hand. "What about Ambrose
Sloan? You aim to fire him, Major?"

"No, I do not," McQuade said sternly. "However, as we
all know, Ambrose Sloan goes strictly by the book. He's
one of those citified, civilized, fancy-Dan lawyers. A good
legal mind but no guts!"

"So what're you aimin' to do?"

"Here's the way I see it," McQuade announced. "Sloan
lost the case because he wasn't willing to fight fire with
fire. The Southern Pacific should have been charged with
every form of collusion known to man. But Sloan played
by gentlemen's rules—and lost—and now we're forced
to await the decision of the Supreme Court. I say we stop
waiting and start fighting—now!"

"Amen to that!" someone shouted. "Where do we start,
Major?"

"We start by hiring Alex Fitzhugh. We'll appoint him

co-counsel with Sloan, for the simple reason we can't afford to dismiss the attorney of record. But Alex won't have
anything to do with Sloan or the Supreme Court. Instead,
we'll turn him loose and let him explore ways to take the
fight to the Southern Pacific. Injunctions, nuisance suits,
conspiracy charges—anything that hits them where it hurts.
Anything that'll make the Octopus squirm!"

Another farmer spoke out. "We're with you till hell
freezes over, Major. But I reckon we're all wonderin' the
same thing. What's Mr. Fitzhugh got to say for hisself?
We'd like to hear his ideas."

"Let's ask him." McQuade turned with an expansive
gesture. "Alex, the floor's all yours. What's your opinion
thus far?"

Tallman replied politely. "Gentlemen, I commend your
spirit and everything you stand for. However, if I may be
permitted to say so, you've got the cart before the horse."

McQuade's brow puckered in a frown. "Would you care
to spell that out?"

"Of course," Tallman said lightly. "Before we can talk
about legal action, I need to examine the case in its entirety.
Otherwise, I'd be operating totally in the dark. So what I
need to hear is your version—a layman's view—of the
Southern Pacific's misdeeds. Then I can determine how to
hit them where it hurts most. Do you see my point?"

"You asked for it," McQuade said with a graveled
chuckle. "We can quote you chapter and verse without
end." He turned back to the crowd. "All right, boys, who
wants the first shot?"

"I do!" A rawboned farmer with a toothy grin jumped
to his feet. "I was one of the first to settle hereabouts.

Hanford weren't no more than a whistlestop when I come west. Hadn't even built the depot—"

"No speeches, Wally," McQuade interrupted. "Get to the point."

"Well, anyway," Wally Branden went on, "I bought my land fair and square. The railroad was askin' two dollars an acre and that's what I paid—cash money!"

Tallman raised an uncertain eyebrow. "Was there any record that money had exchanged hands?"

"Yessir, there was," Branden said morosely. "I got a sales contract signed personal by some bigwig with the Southern Pacific. Hell, ever' man in this room got one! Didn't we, boys?"

There was a gruff murmur of agreement from the crowd. Tallman quieted them with an upraised palm. "One moment, gentlemen! If you obtained a valid contract, then the sale would have been judged legal and binding. What happened to convince the court otherwise?"

"A loophole!" Branden said in an aggrieved tone. "Leastways that's what Ambrose Sloan called it. The contract read that we'd get our deeds once the railroad got title to the government land grants. Only it didn't work that way."

"Wally, lemme tell it!" another farmer broke in. "Mr. Fitzhugh, my name is Iver Kneutson and I'll make it short and simple. Once the railroad got title, we was notified the price had gone up to a hundred dollars an acre. Gawd-damn piece of paper told us to pay up or vacate our farms in thirty days."

"Sonsabitches!" Branden shouted, biting off the words. "After we'd cleared the fields and built houses and barns.

All them improvements, and then they tell us to pay up or get out!"

Tallman shook his head with just the right touch of amazement. "What was your response?"

"Told 'em to go to hell!" Kneutson said. "Then we wrote our congressman and sent along a copy of the sales contract. Later, we found out he was a Southern Pacific man, bought and paid for. Next thing you know the railroad filed an eviction suit in federal district court."

"I see." Tallman pulled at his earlobe, thoughtful. "And that's when you retained Ambrose Sloan—to defend you?"

"For a fact." Kneutson shifted his quid of tobacco to the off cheek. "Only Sloan never told us the straight of it. Turned out the railroad owns the judge. A federal judge!"

Tallman looked dubious. "How can you be sure?"

"Cause we lost," Branden croaked indignantly. "That buttermouth pissant of a judge ruled our sales contracts was invalid. He said the Southern Pacific had legal right to set a price based on fair market value of the land. Jesus Christ! There would't've been no market value unless we'd settled here and built up our farms."

"And it gets worse," Kneutson added furiously. "The railroad's already started advertising improved land for a hundred an acre. Which means they ain't got no doubt about whichaway the Supreme Court's gonna rule. So we either got to pony up or get out—lose everything!"

"The overriding factor," McQuade pointed out, "comes down to simple mathematics. At those prices, we're talking about sixteen thousand dollars for a quarter-section of land. None of us here could beg, borrow or steal that amount of money. The railroad knows it and the price was purposely set skyhigh. In collusion with judges and government officials, the whole affair was rigged to steal our land. To impoverish us by legal edict!"

Tallman pondered on it a moment. Their story had the ring of truth, and he read no guile in their emotional statements. Yet, even for the Southern Pacific, a conspiracy so vast and elaborate was difficult to credit. Then, too, there were the train bombings and blown bridges to consider. Honest settlers, however great the provocation, did not resort to sabotage and terror. Some essential piece of the puzzle was yet to be revealed, and only then would the whole truth emerge. He decided to stall.

"Let me suggest a plan," he ventured. "Any legal action—whether it's an injunction or charges of collusion—will stem from your original agreement with the Southern Pacific. Before we make a move, I'll need to analyze one of these sales contracts. Then we can decide on the best course to follow."

McQuade gave him a quizzical glance. "We've already lost too much time. Won't that just delay matters even further?"

"Only a day or so," Tallman temporized. "It's vital, because everything hinges on the wording of the contract. Perhaps someone would be kind enough to provide me with a copy."

Angela placed a hand on his arm. "I would be most happy to assist you, Mr. Fitzhugh. I have my husband's original contract in a strongbox at home."

Her fingers tightened in a quick squeeze, then she removed her hand. Tallman sensed she had more on her mind than legal matters. He kept his tone casual.

"You're sure it's not too much trouble, Mrs. Pryor?"

"Goodness, no!" Angela's eyes crinkled with a smile. "Anything for the cause, Mr. Fitzhugh."

"Fine," Tallman said affably. "Would sometime tomorrow be convenient?"

"Perfect," Angela agreed. "I'll give you directions to my place. Shall we say early afternoon?"

"By all means, Mrs. Pryor."

McQuade fixed them with a curious look. He seemed on the verge of saying something, then appeared to change his mind. He turned back to the crowd.

"Meeting adjourned till further notice."

SEVEN

Tallman emerged from the café. A noon-hour lull had settled over Hanford, and the town seemed somnolent beneath a warm sun. He lit a cigar and stood for a moment surveying the empty street. Then he walked toward the hotel.

The League meeting still occupied his mind. Despite himself, he was impressed by the arguments put forth by the settlers. Their outrage was genuine, seemingly grounded in the anger of men who believed themselves in the right. Far from the squatters he'd expected, they gave the appearance of law-abiding farmers, hard working and forthright. None of them looked capable of blowing a bridge or derailing a train.

Still, there was no question that acts of violence had been directed at the Southern Pacific. Which led inevitably to speculation about the leader of the Settlers' League. Major Thomas McQuade scarcely looked the part of a farmer. His cut of dress and overbearing manner marked him as a man with only limited experience behind a plow. Nor was he the sort whose ambitions centered on a quarter-section of land and the yearly harvest. In sum and substance, he seemed an unlikely champion of common settlers. His motives would definitely stand for investigation.

Strolling along the boardwalk, Tallman told himself he'd played into luck with Angela Pryor. She struck him as a young widow with hot pants and a pronounced interest in the opposite sex. His appointment with her this afternoon would provide the perfect setting for a bit of probing. Flattery, mixed with discreet interrogation, would shed even more light on the innerworkings of the Settlers' League. There was, moreover, every chance she might afford some insight into the motives of Major Thomas McQuade. In the capacity of recording secretary, her knowledge of the League and its leader was undoubtedly extensive. All in all, she was a valuable source of information, and one to be cultivated in every way possible. If she wanted her weeds plowed, Tallman thought it would be no great effort to oblige her. A woman with a stiff cock in her hand was generally the best of talkers. Once her legs parted all her secrets were laid bare.

A tantalizing picture formed in Tallman's mind. As he approached the hotel, he became intrigued by a vision of Angela Pryor with her legs spread wide. Major McQuade stepped out the door and halted in his path.

"There you are, Alex," McQuade greeted him. "I just stopped by to invite you to lunch."

"Thanks anyway, Major," Tallman responded. "I went down early to beat the crowd. The blue plate special's not bad—meat loaf."

"Join me for a cup of coffee, then."

"Another time," Tallman begged off. "I'm on my way to see Angela Pryor."

"Of course," McQuade said with a bland expression. "She's going to show you her . . . contract."

Tallman caught an inflection in the words. "Are you trying to tell me something, Major?"

"No, no," McQuade said, too quickly. "Although there are times when I regret I'm a happily married man."

"Mrs. Pryor being one of those times?"

"Exactly," McQuade affirmed. "To put it mildly, Angela's very easy on the eyes. I'm amazed she's remained a widow this long."

"How do you account for it?"

"Good common sense," McQuade said forcefully. "She's a woman of property and she can afford to be choosy. She'll make an excellent match for somebody with aspirations."

"Hmmm." Tallman smiled, shook his head. "You're not the local marriage broker, are you, Major?"

"God forbid!" McQuade chortled. "A man could do worse, though. I suspect Angela knows how to keep the home fires burning."

"Well . . ." Tallman hesitated, shrugged. "Where duty's concerned, I'm all business, Major. The fewer complications the better, that's my motto."

"Commendable," McQuade noted dryly. "I'll be interested to hear if Angela has other ideas."

"A gentleman never tells. Having served as a Union officer, I'm certain you'll agree it's the only honorable way."

"What makes you think I was a Union man?"

"Your accent," Tallman said easily. "I'd place it some-where in the midwest. Minnesota or perhaps Illinois."

"Close," McQuade admitted. "I commanded a battal-ion of Ohio volunteers."

"What brought you to California?"

"What else?" McQuade laughed. "The land of opportu-nity! At the time, of course, I wasn't aware it was owned lock, stock and barrel by the Southern Pacific."

Tallman grinned. "Maybe we'll still find a way to up-set their applecart."

"That's the spirit. You go on out to Angela's and study that contract. Let me know what you turn up."

"You can count on it, Major."

McQuade directed him to the local livery stable. There, after dickering briefly on price, Tallman hired a horse and buggy. A short while later he turned north out of town onto a farm road. He was pondering yet another aspect in the overall riddle.

For a farmer, Thomas McQuade spent a lot of time in town. And there was no dirt beneath his fingernails. It made for interesting speculation.

A swollen ball of orange dipped westward toward the hori-zon. The river was molten with sunlight, and to the east, the Sierra Nevadas were bathed in a spectral glow. The tranquil scene belied the violent nature of those who inhabited the land.

Tallman was frankly surprised by the countryside. The eastern quadrant of valley was watered by swift-running mountain streams. Everywhere he looked a latticework of irrigation ditches fanned out from the Kings River and lesser tributaries. The settlers had clearly invested years of back-breaking labor in channeling water to their fields. The results were apparent in the ripe summer abundance of produce. Wheat and barley, sugar beets and all manner of vegetables covered the land as far as the eye could see. Here and there small herds of cattle grazed placidly on fenced grassland. The whole was a picture of hard-earned prosperity, and permanence.

All across the valley was a sense of people who had traveled far and planted their roots deep. Angela Pryor's farm was typical of those Tallman passed on his drive northward. The main house was a one-story structure, neatly whitewashed with green shutters and a long porch on the front. Flowers bordered the house in a wild profusion of colors, and a stone walkway skirted the edge of a manicured lawn. Out behind there was a large red barn, flanked by a stock tank and an open-sided machinery shed. There was nothing about the farm to suggest squatters, or anarchists. It looked fit for a country squire.

Angela met Tallman at the door. She was dressed in a gingham gown that clung to her like wet paint. Her hair was upswept in a mass of golden curls and she smelled wonderously fresh, as though she'd just stepped from a lavender-scented bath. Her cheeks were lightly rouged and her hazel eyes shone. An aura of verve and bubbling gaiety seemed to surround her as she opened the screen door. She greeted him with an enchanting smile.

"Welcome to my home, Alex."

"The pleasure's all mine, Mrs. Pryor."

"Please," she said softly. "Call me Angela. I do hate formality, don't you?"

"I do indeed . . . Angela."

She took his hat and hung it on a halltree. Then, with a sort of bustling vitality, she led him into the parlor. The room was handsomely appointed, with several armchairs, a burgandy satin sofa and brightly patterned curtains on the windows. Vases, filled with freshly cut flowers, were scattered about in a rainbow of colors. On a low table, which stood before the sofa, was a china tea service and a decanter of brandy. She waved him away from one of the armchairs and guided him instead to the sofa. She seated herself within arm's reach and smiled engagingly.

"May I offer you a refreshment? I have imported Oriental tea, fresh off the boat from San Francisco. Or if you prefer, I have a fine Napoleon brandy."

"Brandy would do nicely, thank you."

"Oh, good!" Angela exclaimed. "I'm partial to a nip now and then myself. You won't tell anyone, will you?"

"Consider my lips sealed."

"I just knew you were a progressive thinker. So many men are stuffy about things like that. Honestly, it's worth a woman's reputation to take a single drop!"

Angela set out two glasses, which were delicately overlaid with silver, and expertly poured from the decanter. Watching her, Tallman saw that she was charged with excitement. Her eyes were glittery and her every word was spoken with a slight tremor. There was, moreover, a sense of high-strung expectation in her manner. He thought it had nothing to do with the business of the Settlers' League.

Instead, the flowers and brandy, along with her vivacious chatter, were intended to create an atmosphere. He smiled inwardly, amused that she'd set the stage for a seduction. He decided to let her make the first move.

Attentive to her small talk, Tallman subtly lavished her with praise. He complimented her on her home and the furnishings, and left no doubt that he considered her a gracious hostess. She responded to the flattery, and by their third brandy the byplay had turned cozy and intimate. Abruptly, as though he'd forgotten the purpose of his visit, he raised the subject of the Southern Pacific contract. His tone implied business before pleasure, and contained a hint of promise. Somewhat reluctantly, she left the room and returned moments later with a sheaf of papers. Her attitude indicated that her own priorities were along more personal lines.

Tallman quickly scanned the contract. The content of the document was framed in the convoluted legalese typically employed by lawyers. For the most part, it was a standard sales agreement and noteworthy only for its obtuse phrasing. Yet one paragraph caught his eye, and he scrutinized it with painstaking care. Once deciphered, the legal jargon was a masterpiece of ambiguity. The paragraph stipulated that the sale would be deemed null and void unless the railroad provided the buyer with a valid deed. Seemingly worded to protect the buyer, the actual intent was something altogether different. By withholding the deed, the Southern Pacific retained the option of canceling the sales agreement. There was no time limit and the railroad was not obligated to establish justification for its action. Nor was there any legal recourse, or any means of redress, spelled out for the buyer. In short, it was a loophole crafted solely for the benefit of the seller.

Stunned, Tallman's eyes narrowed as comprehension seeped through. He appeared calm and collected, but the truth whipped through his mind like jackstraws blown in a high wind. With an almost grudging sense of realization, he knew the Southern Pacific had rigged the scheme from the outset. The settlers were gullible and unversed in legal matters, the perfect suckers. One paragraph, innocuous on the face of it, simply overturned all their rights under the agreement. The railroad could dispossess them at will.

Still another element of the scheme was abundantly clear. The campaign to evict the settlers in Kings County was merely a test case. Should the railroad succeed—with an affirmative ruling by the Supreme Court—a precedent would be established. The next step, quite obviously, would be to dispossess farmers throughout the whole of California. Then the land could be resold, at a vastly inflated price, to a horde of new settlers. The upshot would be millions in added profit for the Southern Pacific.

Tallman felt a sudden loathing for his employer. At the same time, he was nagged by an apparent contradiction. Major Thomas McQuade was no fool, and most certainly realized that the League's position was indefensible. So why had he led the settlers into a futile battle with the railroad? It was a question worth exploring.

After considering a moment, Tallman laid the contract on the table. Then, almost as though he was thinking out loud, he turned to Angela. "The major was right. We'll have to fight fire with fire."

"Do you see some way to force the railroad's hand?"

"Perhaps," Tallman said absently. "It all depends on how tough a game the Major wants to play."

"Don't worry, then," Angela assured him. "Tom McQuade has no intention of losing this fight. We all count our lucky stars he moved to Hanford and organized the Settlers' League."

"Oh?" Tallman inquired innocently. "I just assumed he was one of the original settlers. When did he move to Hanford?"

"Last year," Angela confided. "He moved here from Bakersfield shortly after he bought the old Clarkson farm."

"Clarkson," Tallman mused. "Was he one of the original land buyers?"

Angela gave him a bright little nod. "Clarkson sold out just after the trouble started. And thank God for that! Without Tom McQuade we might never have gotten ourselves organized."

"Maybe it was fate," Tallman observed neutrally. "After all, the Major brought himself a peck of trouble along with a farm. Talk about coincidence."

"Yes, but he never shirked. He jumped into the fight hammer and tongs, and took over when no one else was willing. We owe him an eternal debt of gratitude."

"I guess that makes it mutual. The Major's one of your most ardent admirers. Told me so himself, only this morning."

A look of catlike eagerness appeared in Angela's eyes. "And you, Alex? Are you an admirer, too?"

"Nooo," Tallman said with a waggish grin. "An admirer keeps a respectful distance. I'm finding that increasingly difficult."

"Are you?" Angela said on an indrawn breath. "What do you suggest we do about it?"

Tallman laughed and stretched out his hand. She took it and scooted across the sofa. He put his arm around her and pulled her into a tight embrace, staring raptly into her eyes. Then he kissed her and her mouth parted and their tongues intertwined in a mating dance. She moaned, squirming closer, and ground herself against the hard knot in his groin. Her breathing suddenly quickened in tempo.

Hastily, fumbling with buttons and stays, they undressed each other. Stark naked, they kissed and caressed, locked tightly together. His hand went to the curly blond patch between her legs and his finger slipped easily into her yielding wetness. She grasped his cock, fondling and stroking until it stood erect and pulsating. Then, disengaging from his embrace, she dropped off the sofa and went to her knees. She spread his legs and lowered her head into his crotch. While she stroked with her hand, she laved his balls with the pink tip of her tongue. His manhood stiffened harder, throbbing and engorged with blood.

Leaning forward, he lifted her to her feet and wedged his knees between her legs. Upright, standing over him, her figure was breathtaking. Full rounded hips tapered to a slim waist and rose to coral-tipped jutting breasts. She stared down at him with smoky eyes, heavy-lidded and smoldering with sensuality. Her mouth was agape and her flat stomach rippled with need as she stood there waiting. He ran his hands up her flanks and cupped her breasts in his palms. Then, ever so gently, he began kneading her nipples between thumb and forefinger. She groaned and her eyes closed and her legs went rubbery. His hands grasped her hips and he lowered her downward. He impaled her with a sharp upward thrust.

A gasp parted her lips and her eyes popped open with a wild, feverish look. She straddled him, her knees planted on the sofa, and rammed the head of his cock deep within her moist bog. She pumped up and down, faster and faster, rotating with a rhythmic motion on the downward stroke. He gripped her haunches, guiding her, and bucked upward to meet her in an agonized clash of loins. She lunged and shuddered and her nails raked long welts across his shoulders. He suddenly stood, holding her buttocks firmly in his hands, and drove the whole of himself to her inner depths. Her legs locked around his back and her body jolted with a series of twitching spasms. He exploded within her, and as the scalding rush flooded her insides, she uttered a squeal like a dying rabbit. Then she collapsed, pressed tightly against his chest, and clung to him limp and quivering. He sat down on the sofa, still hard within her dampness, and cradled her in his arms. She buried her face in the hollow of his shoulder, completely drained. Her mouth moved in a low, guttural cry.

Later, when she'd recovered her voice, they talked again of McQuade and the Settlers' League. She told him everything he wanted to know.

EIGHT

Tallman pulled into Fresno shortly after midnight. The bright lights and general hubbub of the sporting district made it simple to locate. Where Elm Street intersected Broadway, he stepped down from the buggy and tied the horse to a hitching-rail. Then he went looking for Vivian.

Some hours earlier, Tallman had escaped the clutches of Angela Pryor. After their talk, she'd cooked him supper and treated him to more of her fine Napoleon brandy. When she suggested he spend the night, he had begged off and got her to settle for an encore performance in the sack. Their second time around, she had proved herself an accomplished gymnast on a goose-down mattress. Upon leaving, he'd felt a little used and bruised. The widow Pryor was of the rough and tumble lovemaking school.

By a roundabout route, Tallman had then headed for Fresno. Angela's unwitting disclosures about McQuade and the Settlers' League had unveiled new facets of the case. With all he'd learned, it was therefore imperative that he brief Vivian immediately. Then, too, it was no less vital that he obtain a report on what she had unearthed in Fresno.

An exchange of information might very well suggest some quicker approach to their investigation. There was, moreover, the matter of Ambrose Sloan. He meant to sic Vivian on the lawyer without delay.

Fresno's sporting district was slowly winding down for the night. Tallman bypassed the sleezier dives and limited his search to those establishments with a touch of class. His third stop was the Palace Variety Theater, and he spotted Vivian the moment he walked through the door. She was seated at a table with two men, one portly and the other trim. By their attire, he pegged them as men of substance and some position in the community. He walked to the bar and took a place directly opposite Vivian's table. Ordering rye, he casually turned with the glass in hand and put his back to the counter. He sipped and willed Vivian to look in his direction.

To all appearances, a contest was underway at the table. The stout man and the dandy were obviously in a neck-to-neck race for Vivian's favor. She, in turn, was acting the coquette, playing one off against the other with minxish charm. She laughed, quaffing their champagne with gusto, and divided her attention equally between them. At last, her head thrown back in a bawdy howl of merriment, her eyes drifted to the bar. She did a quick double take and her gaze fastened on Tallman. He ducked his chin, acknowledging her look, and cut his eyes sharply toward the door. She flashed a pearly grin in return and instantly went back to the courting ritual with her gentlemen friends. Tallman finished his drink, watching the chorus line onstage with jaded disinterest. Then he sauntered to the door and stepped outside.

An hour or so later the Palace closed for the night. Posted in a doorway across the street, Tallman observed Vivian's admirers depart as the theater emptied. Shortly afterwards, Vivian emerged with several other girls and bid them a loud good night. Turning uptown, she walked off alone and strolled toward the distant intersection. Tallman hung back a moment, then trailed her from the opposite side of the street. On Broadway, she rounded the corner and went directly to her hotel.

Tallman angled across the street. He moved through the hotel entrance and saw Vivian waiting at the bottom of the stairway. She pressed a finger to her lips and then pointed to the night clerk, who was snoozing peacefully behind the desk. Tallman crossed the lobby and followed her to the second floor landing. There she proceeded along the hall to her room and unlocked the door. Without a word, he slipped inside and halted in the dark. She closed the door and locked it behind her.

Vivian turned and he took her in his arms. She kissed him long and hungrily, performing a variation of bumps and grinds against his groin. Finally, with a low chuckle, he broke her hold and swatted her smartly on the rump. She laughed and moved to the washstand, tossing her cape on the bed. A match flared and she lit a lamp, adjusting the wick to a dim glow. She pirouetted around and spread her arms in a grandiose gesture.

"However humble, there's no place like home!"

"Christ," Tallman muttered, eyeballing the stark furnishings. "I told you to pick a fleabag, not a flophouse."

"All part of the charade," Vivian said cheerily. "Even the girls at the Palace think I'm busted flat. One of them offered to loan me ten dollars till payday. How's that for acting the part?"

Tallman inspected the room closely. "Offhand, I'd say this dump would convince anyone."

"You ain't seen nothin' yet!" Vivian hooted. "Wait till the cockroaches start their parade."

"Spare me the details." Tallman sat down in the single straight-backed chair. "We've got work to do and damned little time. I have to be back in Hanford before daylight."

Vivian's expression turned serious. She took a seat on the edge of the bed, hands folded in her lap. "I'm all ears. You talk and I'll listen."

Tallman related the events of the past two days. He skipped over nothing and he dwelled at length on the more salient points. He briefed her on McQuade and the Settlers' League meeting, and outlined details of the Southern Pacific sales contract. Only one omission was made in his recounting. He neglected to mention his bruising tryst with the widow Pryor.

"In a nutshell," he concluded, "the railroad's out to screw the settlers. Which means we were conned from the very beginning. Our assignment has nothing whatever to do with squatters. We were hired to make sure those people got screwed six ways to Sunday."

"So it appears," Vivian allowed. "Of course, we're in no position to make any judgments. We're private detectives for hire, not idealists."

"Once before I told you the Southern Pacific has the law on its side, and nothing has happened to change that. We're still the mercenaries and we'll earn our pay. But I'm starting to think it's a helluva way to make a living."

"Unless I missed something"—Vivian paused for emphasis—"the Southern Pacific isn't the only villain in the piece. From what you say, there are other forces at work."

"No doubt about it," Tallman growled. "And it's dirty work of the lowest kind. I'm convinced someone is using those farmers as a stalking horse. Or perhaps it would be more accurate to say a sacrificial goat."

"To what purpose?" Vivian asked. "Who would benefit by sabotaging bridges and trains?"

"Good question," Tallman said grumpily. "I haven't the foggiest notion."

"But you suspect McQuade?"

"So far as I can determine, he's the only candidate."

"And his motive?"

"One big blank," Tallman said, troubled. "For all Angela Pryor told me, the man's still an absolute cipher."

"Not entirely," Vivian reminded him. "You know McQuade organized the Settlers' League, and without him it would fall apart. I gather he's not the Good Samaritan type, and that tells us a great deal in itself. He has to have a reason, some way he'll benefit. Otherwise, what's the point?"

"I admit I'm stumped," Tallman conceded. "For a moment it occurred to me that he might be an agent for the railroad. Wrecking trains and blowing bridges certainly casts the settlers in a bad light. But on second thought, I decided the theory won't hold water. That's just a little too smooth, even for the Southern Pacific."

"If not the railroad, then who?"

"Try asking me a *simple* question."

"All right," Vivian replied with a wave of her hand.

"Why did he move from Bakersfield to Hanford? All the more important, why did he make the move at the exact time the Southern Pacific served eviction notice on the settlers?"

"I'll go you one better," Tallman countered. "Why would he buy a farm when he knew he wouldn't receive a valid deed? To compound matters, he must have known that the sales contract with the railroad wasn't worth the paper it's written on."

"Coincidence?" Vivian offered. "Poor judgment?"

"Some coincidence." Tallman scoffed. "And it goddamn sure wasn't poor judgment. McQuade's no fool, and only an imbecile would have bought into that kind of fight. His move there was planned—premeditated."

"You're saying he bought into the fight for a purpose?"

"I see no other explanation."

"Which means we've come full circle."

Tallman stared at her a long time, finally he drew a deep breath. "It's like a Chinese puzzle. A box within a box within a box."

"Why not ask McQuade himself—point-blank?"

"Ask him what?"

"Why he moved to Hanford and bought the farm."

"I already have," Tallman remarked. "I got him talking, and he told me he'd come west from Ohio. Went into a song and dance about California being the land of opportunity. He very pointedly said nothing—zero—about having settled first in Bakersfield."

Vivian whistled softly under her breath. "He's a man of many secrets, our Major McQuade."

"Well, as some poet so aptly penned—'O what a tangled web we weave when first we practice to deceive.' Our job is to find a strand and unravel the Major's web."

"Where do you suggest we start?"

"Here." Tallman gestured out the window. "That's why I busted my arse getting to Fresno tonight."

"Fresno?" Vivian repeated blankly. "You think we'll find the answer in Fresno?"

"You'll recall I mentioned a Fresno lawyer who represents the Settlers' League. His name is Sloan."

"Sloan?" Vivian looked astounded. "Not Ambrose Sloan?"

"How'd you know that?"

"Call it dumb luck," Vivian said honestly. "The two gents I was sitting with tonight, when you gave me the high sign . . . remember?"

Tallman searched his memory. "One was fat and somewhere in his late forties. The other was slim and quite well-dressed, probably ten years younger."

"You don't miss a trick," Vivian said with genuine wonder. "Well, hold onto your hat, lover! The younger one was Ambrose Sloan."

Tallman smiled, obviously pleased. "Tell me about it."

"I figured somebody prosperous would be the best source of information. So I collared those two and gave them the Jezebel treatment. The fat one's Benjamin Canby, president of the Mercantile National Bank." Vivian suddenly burst out laughing. "You might say they're in a dead heat to see who gets into my pants first."

"What have you learned so far?"

"Not much," Vivian explained. "Too much curiosity too fast would have seemed out of character for a saloon girl. I was working up to it gradually."

Tallman considered a moment. "All right, here's the way we'll work it. Ditch the banker and concentrate on Sloan. Be discreet, but pump him dry. I want specifics on his connection with McQuade."

"You think they're in cahoots?"

"Something smells fishy," Tallman said with assurance. "By all accounts, Sloan is a capable attorney. But he took on a hopeless case and I suspect he knew it from the outset. One look at that sales contract would have convinced anyone with even a little legal training."

Vivian made an empty gesture with her hands. "Maybe he was trying to bluff the Southern Pacific into a settlement. Or maybe he just saw the chance to earn a sizable fee. Lawyers are known for their sticky palms."

"Or maybe," Tallman added, frowning heavily, "he's involved in a little hocus-pocus with McQuade. I get suspicious when someone badmouths their own attorney. And McQuade personally handpicked Sloan."

"So you want me to find out the score?"

"Exactly."

"Will do," Vivian said agreeably. "Anything to speed the case along—and get me out of Fresno!"

"What's wrong with Fresno?"

"A horny bastard named Horace Logan. He owns the theater, and a girl either puts out or she loses her job. I can't hold him off much longer."

"Then the quicker the better with Sloan. Turn on the charm and get him to talk."

A funny look surfaced in Vivian's eyes. "Was that how you got the widow Pryor to talk?"

"Well . . ." Tallman gave her a sheepish smile. "Ask me no questions and I'll tell you no lies. Fair enough?"

"On one condition!" Vivian studied him with a wicked expression. "Share and share alike . . . equal treatment!"

Tallman groaned and consulted his pocket watch. "We're a little short on time."

"I've got a short fuse." Vivian brightened with a wide smile.

Tallman wanted nothing more than a good night's sleep. He was numb and overworked, and he thought another roll in the hay might cripple him. Yet he heard the siren's call in her voice, and temptation beckoned. He rose to the occasion.

On the bed, Vivian hugged him with fierce possession. Her arms clutched him about the neck and her breasts flattened against his chest. She kissed him passionately and trembled with an almost uncontrollable sense of urgency. Her hand unbuttoned the fly of his trousers and groped for his cock. She stroked it tenderly, lovingly, her caress like the gentle tingle of a snowflake.

Tallman got back to Hanford later than he'd planned.

NINE

Tallman shaved with dulled concentration. He stared at himself in the mirror. He'd dipped his wick once too often last night and it showed. His eyes were bloodshot and scratchy and felt curiously like burnt-out holes. The mirror told the story in vivid detail.

Groggy from the long night, he wielded the razor with a careful hand. He'd had no sleep and nothing that faintly resembled rest. Between hopping about from bed to bed, he'd traveled almost a hundred miles. Only an hour ago, with false dawn lighting the sky, he had returned the horse and buggy to the stable. Now, after a bird bath and a shave, it was apparent there would be no immediate restorative effects. His head pounded like an ore crusher and the mere thought of pussy made his rod throb like a toothache. He toyed with the idea of quitting Pinkerton and entering another line of work. The detective business was sometimes a ballbreaker—literally.

A knock sounded at the door as he wiped lather from his face. He dropped the towel on the washstand and padded barefoot to the bed. He was in his undershorts and hardly expecting company, particularly with the sun only an hour high. His shoulder rig hung draped on the headboard and he slipped the Colt clear. Then he moved to the door.

"Yes?"

"It's me, Mr. Fitzhugh. Bob Simpson, from the desk."

Tallman cracked open the door. The hotel owner peered through the slit with a silly grin. He jerked a thumb down the hallway.

"Major McQuade sent me up with a message."

"A message?"

"He wants to know if you'll join him for breakfast."

"Of course," Tallman said automatically. "Is he waiting downstairs?"

"No, he went on to the café. Told me to tell you to meet him there."

"Thanks, Bob," Tallman said with a bogus smile. "I'll be along shortly."

"No trouble, Mr. Fitzhugh. Always glad to oblige the major."

Tallman waved and closed the door. He marked again that McQuade spent an inordinate amount of time in town for a farmer. As for the breakfast invitation, the purpose was all too transparent. McQuade clearly wanted to grill him about the Southern Pacific sales contract. How much he'd learned would be a matter of vital interest to the League leader. And his answers might very well affect McQuade's future plans.

While he dressed, Tallman mulled on it further. He decided it would be a mistake to try second-guessing McQuade. The better approach was to play it straight, without guile or pretense. His qualms about the contract itself should be expressed openly and with the proper degree of amazement. Even his opinion regarding Ambrose Sloan should be broached frankly, with just a dash of professional outrage. Only on the subject of McQuade's farm—purchased without a deed—would he avoid any direct reply. He mustn't let on that Angela Pryor had talked too much. Or risk letting slip what he now suspected.

A few minutes later Tallman entered the café. McQuade was seated at a window table, nursing a mug of coffee. He rose with a smile and an outstretched hand.

"Good morning, Alex."

"Morning, Major." Tallman returned his handshake with a slow grin. "You must get up with the chickens."

"Old army habits," McQuade said, motioning him to a chair. "Are you hungry?"

"Famished would be more like it."

"No doubt." McQuade chortled out loud. "I understand you had a long night."

"Oh?" Tallman lifted an eyebrow. "Somebody carrying tales?"

"Hanford's too small for secrets. Bob Simpson almost burst his britches the minute I walked in the hotel. Told me you'd come dragging in with the sunrise."

"Dragging?" Tallman parroted with amusement. "Well, I suppose it's a fair description. I've certainly felt peppier."

A waitress appeared and took their orders. Tallman opted for ham and eggs with a stack of flapjacks. McQuade, sticking to simpler fare, asked for biscuits covered with red-eye gravy. The girl brought Tallman a mug of coffee, which did wonders for his fuzzy vision. He expected the conversation to shift to the Southern Pacific; but for once his instincts failed him. McQuade hunched forward with a faintly lascivious grin.

"How was it?"

"Beg pardon?"

"Angela," McQuade said eagerly. "I know you spent the night with her. Is she as hot as she looks?"

"Why . . ." Tallman faltered, never more amazed. "You surprise me, Major. I thought we agreed a gentleman never tells."

"I know," McQuade said with a hangdog look. "But there are exceptions, Alex. After all, if it wasn't for me you wouldn't have met her."

"And I appreciate—"

"Not only that," McQuade hurried on. "You wouldn't have been invited to her house . . . or allowed to sleep over."

"True."

"So you might say I'm your benefactor. And quite frankly, I've always been intrigued by Angela. Forbidden fruit and all that—normal curiosity."

Tallman suddenly realized he was talking to a closet voyeur. McQuade had probably never had his pole greased outside the marriage bed. A strange piece of ass and a glass of ice water would doubtless give him a stroke. He got his kicks by the vicarious route, acting out his sexual fantasies through the escapades of others. Tallman decided to play on the weakness.

"You wouldn't repeat anything I said, would you, Major?"

"Never!" McQuade swore. "On my word as an officer and a gentleman."

Tallman let his gaze drift off, as though reliving some moment of profound ecstasy. "She's all woman, Major. Hotter than a three dollar pistol. Would you believe it?— She actually copped my joint."

"She what?"

"Went down on me." Tallman said with a rolling laugh. "Sucked the lollipop to the very last drop."

McQuade fairly drooled. "Then what?"

"Well . . ." Tallman baited him with a conspiratorial look. "You're sure you wouldn't talk out of school?"

"Not a word."

"I'm straight arrow myself," Tallman whispered, darting a glance at nearby diners. "But Angela's a lady with very peculiar tastes. So we had ourselves an old-fashioned Roman circus. Head to toe, cunnilingus and fellatio—all we could eat and more."

"You—" McQuade's mouth went pasty. "You did *that?*"

"Surprised myself." Tallman said with feigned wonder. "She turned me into a regular muff diver. And damned if I didn't like it."

McQuade's eyes lighted up as though he'd heard a new verse in an old sermon. "What happened next?"

"Then we played stink finger and hide the wienie."

"How's that again?"

"I tickled her rosebud till she was about to explode."

"Yes . . .?"

"Then I stuck it to her so deep her tonsils rattled."

McQuade cleared his throat. "How many times?"

"Not bragging," Tallman said almost idly, "but I lost count somewhere around four or five."

"Five." McQuade swallowed hard. "Good God! No wonder her husband died an early death."

"Tell you a secret, Major." Tallman rocked his hand, fingers splayed. "I've been fucked in my day—from virgins to whores—but never like that. Angela Pryor's in a class all by herself."

The waitress materialized with their breakfast platters. McQuade fell silent and attacked his gravy-soaked biscuits like a ravenous dog. Watching him, Tallman thought the gambit had worked out rather well. Though highly exaggerated, his salacious account had distracted McQuade from the Southern Pacific. The major was clearly a man who got his jollies listening to dirty talk and clinical tales of fornication. It was a device not to be overlooked in the days ahead. A word here and there about Angela Pryor would serve to divert McQuade and keep his mind occupied. And all the while the investigation would go forward.

After breakfast, McQuade seemed to have recovered his composure. He swigged a second mug of coffee and made no further reference to things sexual. Instead, once more austere and overbearing, the turnabout in his character was startling. He studied Tallman with a kind of bemused objectivity.

"Now that you've examined the contract"—he let the thought dangle a moment—"how do you suggest we proceed?"

The question caught Tallman unprepared. He'd expected an interrogation about the settlers' legal position, some test of his ethical code. Apparently McQuade had concluded that anyone with the morals of a tomcat was worthy of trust. So it was down to business, quid pro quo. A mutual scratching of backs.

"I'll need a bit of time," Tallman said with a shrug. "From a legal standpoint, that contract forecloses most of our options. So I'll have to pull something out of a hat—fabricate new charges."

"Do whatever needs doing." McQuade's tone was severe. "But have a plan worked out within the next couple of days."

"Any special reason for the time limit?"

"I'm catching the morning train to Bakersfield. I expect to be back the day after tomorrow. See to it you've pulled something out of the hat by then."

Tallman was instantly attentive. "What's in Bakersfield?"

"Personal business." An indirection came into McQuade's eyes. "Nothing that concerns the Settlers' League."

"Need a good lawyer?" Tallman gave him a tired smile. "I work cheap and I'm not exactly overburdened with clients."

McQuade sidestepped the question. "For the time being, concentrate on the Southern Pacific. Do the job right and you'll have all the clients you can handle."

On the spur of the moment Tallman decided to tail him to Bakersfield. Something in McQuade's cryptic manner told him it was the smart move. There was, moreover, the fact that McQuade was originally from Bakersfield. Which lent added significance to the trip. A surveillance might easily uncover an old strand in the web of deception. And perhaps a motive.

Outside the café, Tallman took his leave. He hurried back to his hotel room and threw his suitcase on the bed. One side of the bag was equipped with a false bottom; within the compartment was all the paraphernalia for operating in disguise. He stripped to his undershorts and went to work before the washstand mirror. A vial of stage makeup and a bottle of spirit gum turned the trick. Within a matter of minutes, he was swarthy in appearance and a brushy mustache was pasted onto his upper lip. The transformation was complete when he donned a battered slouch hat, a baggy pair of trousers, and an oversized jacket. A final inspection in the mirror told the tale. Ash Tallman, otherwise known as Alex Fitzhugh, had ceased to exist. In his place stood a careworn bum who wouldn't draw a second glance.

A half hour later Tallman boarded the train for Bakersfield. He'd slipped out of the hotel by the rear firestairs and made his way to the depot. There he'd loitered around until McQuade took a seat in the lead passenger coach. Then he mounted the steps to the rear coach and found himself a window seat. He settled back and tugged the slouch hat down over his eyes.

He was asleep when the morning southbound chugged out of Hanford.

Late that afternoon the train rumbled to a halt in Bakersfield. Tallman was rested and alert, revitalized by his extended nap. He watched out the window as McQuade crossed the platform and disappeared around the corner of the stationhouse. Then he quickly detrained and tagged along.

Tallman was an old hand at surveillance. He maintained a discreet distance from the subject, and regardless of the surroundings, he managed to make himself all but invisible. Sometimes he shadowed the man from the opposite side of the street and sometimes he tailed directly behind. He was never too close to be spotted and never too far to be ditched. He stuck like a leech, unshakable.

Within a block it became apparent McQuade was on no ordinary business trip. His every effort seemed directed at throwing off a tail. He ducked into a pool hall, only to reappear on the street not thirty seconds later. He stood for a moment, surveying passersby, and then walked away. A few blocks farther on he entered an emporium and slowly browsed through the store. Then he emerged by a side door and marched off at a rapid pace. Once in the downtown area, he mingled with shoppers and all but lost himself in the crowd. He appeared to have no fixed destination.

Tallman took it all in stride. Over the years, he'd seen every trick in the book, and nothing phased him for long. Yet he was quick to admit that McQuade was a cute piece of work, clearly versed in the more serious aspects of hide and seek. The game ended on the far side of town, a block from the central business district. McQuade rounded a corner, momentarily disappearing from view, and then abruptly reversed directions. Tallman veered into a saloon the instant McQuade reappeared around the corner. He waited by a flyblown window as the League leader passed the saloon and angled sharply across the street. He saw McQuade enter a building and somehow sensed the chase was over. A sign on the storefront window caught his eye.

KERN COUNTY LAND & DEVELOPMENT CO.
Harlan Ordway
President

Staring at the sign, Tallman considered a knotty problem. The land company, beyond any doubt, represented a strand in the web. Yet the longer he shadowed McQuade, the greater the risk of being recognized and blowing his cover. On sudden impulse, he decided to return to Hanford by the night train. There, once more in the guise of Alex Fitzhugh, he would make further inquiries into the League leader's background. Then, when McQuade returned home, he would create some pretext to leave town. Trains were frequent and Bakersfield wasn't that far away. His investigation of the land company could then be conducted with leisurely attention to details.

Not the least of which was the one named Harlan Ordway.

TEN

The Palace was packed with the usual evening crowd. The barroom was mobbed and it was already standing room only in the theater. Only one table was empty, located down front with a ringside view of the stage. A reserved sign and a watchful bouncer kept it unoccupied.

Vivian was posted near the broad entranceway to the theater. Her spangled gown revealed the swell of her breasts at the top and the lissome curve of her legs at the bottom. A steady parade of men ogled her with covetous glances, and some of the bolder ones paused to offer a drink. She put them off with a smile and the coy promise of another time. Her attention was fixed on the front door and her gaze was that of a huntress. She was waiting for Ambrose Sloan.

Outwardly gay and effervescent, Vivian was nonetheless troubled. Her meeting with Tallman last night had raised a sticky problem. He wanted her to concentrate on Sloan and play the femme fatale. Yet that presented the nettlesome chore of separating Sloan from Benjamin Canby. The two men always arrived and departed together, like a chummy duo with their own exclusive club. At first, she'd thought they were queer; but events had quickly dispelled that notion. Both men wanted her and each was hesitant of making a move for fear of offending the other. Friendship, judging from their behavior, was stronger than lust. Still, it was imperative that she cleave them apart before she put the whammy on Sloan. Three was definitely a crowd for what she had in mind.

"How's the new girl tonight?"

Vivian turned to confront another of her problems. Horace Logan, the theater owner, stood with his thumbs hooked in his vest. He eyed her with the proprietary air of a sultan inspecting his harem. His breath smelled like he'd had supper with a vulture.

"Evening, boss!" Vivian faked a carefree smile. "Looks like we've got a full house."

"Lotta good it does you," Logan said with heavy humor. "You act like you're waitin' on a streetcar."

Vivian laughed. "Well, you know me, boss. I'm partial to highrollers. Champagne suits my style better than John Barleycorn."

"I take it you mean Canby and Sloan?"

"Nobody else."

"Time's money," Logan said importantly. "Get your fanny in gear and push a few drinks while you're waitin'."

"C'mon, be a sport," Vivian mewed. "I hustle a bigger tab than any girl in the joint. And it's all because I've got a couple of swells hooked solid. Jeezus, talk about a regular meal ticket."

"Guess again," Logan corrected her. "You are lookin'

your meal ticket square in the kisser. None other than yours truly."

"Criminy sakes." Vivian seemed properly abashed. "Nobody ever said otherwise, boss. You're ace high in my book."

"You could've fooled me," Logan huffed. "You been here three days and you haven't come near my office. Or maybe you accidentally-on-purpose forgot our deal?"

"Nosirree!" Vivian proclaimed. "Sally Randolph never goes back on a promise. I'll show you a good time—real soon."

"How soon?"

"Don't you fret. Keep your couch warm and—"

Vivian saw Canby and Sloan walk through the door. She blew Logan a kiss and hurried toward the front of the barroom. There she linked arms with the two men, smiling radiantly, and steered them toward the theater. A bouncer joined the entourage and cleared a path through the crowd. With the fanfare reserved for big spenders, they were escorted to the vacant ringside table. Hardly were they seated when a waiter appeared with a bucket of iced champagne. He popped the cork and poured with a flourish. Onstage a scruffy band of acrobats bounded out and went into their routine. The crowd quickly lost interest in the newly arrived trio down front.

The mood at the table was lighthearted. Canby and Sloan, who considered themselves bon vivants, ignored the stage show and concentrated on Vivian. Between sips of champagne, they eagle-eyed her peek-a-boo gown and vied with one another in delivering witty remarks. Vivian buttered them up shamelessly and kept a smile plastered on her face. Yet, all the while they clowned for her benefit, she was in something of a quandary. By hook or crook, she had to split them apart, and she was admittedly at a loss for a solution. Sloan wouldn't risk offending Canby, and to provoke an incident herself might very well alienate both men. Finally, stumped for an answer, she decided it was now or never. Time was at a premium, and the urgency of the case overshadowed all else. She spiked the first wedge with blunt directness.

"Ambrose?"

"Yes, my dear?"

"Are you married?"

"Why, no," Sloan replied, somewhat taken aback. "Why do you ask?"

"Oh, just because," Vivan pouted. "You've never invited me out and I'm really a little hurt you haven't tried. Are you ashamed to be seen with me?"

"Quite the contrary," Sloan said stoutly. "Unless it's escaped your notice, I find you extremely attractive. I'd gladly take you anywhere."

"Well, then?" Vivian persisted. "Why haven't you asked? I'm certainly not playing hard to get."

"Hold on!" Canby interrupted. "What about me? Don't I deserve some consideration, too?"

"Now really, Benjamin." Vivian wagged a finger at him. "You're a married man. Anyone would know that."

"How would they know?"

"Silly man!" Vivian giggled. "It's written all over you. You just *look* married."

"What if I am?" Canby demanded. "Why should that stop you from going out with me?"

"Honestly." Vivian looked shocked. "A girl does have to watch her reputation."

"Bullfeathers!" Canby declared hotly. "Your reputation's not all that lily pure. Not working in a dive like this."

"No, it's not." Vivian hesitated, then hammered the spike home. "But you're much too old for me, Benjamin. Why, mercy sakes, you probably have daughters my age!"

A strained stillness fell over the table. Canby's face turned red as oxblood and he glowered at her in tonguetied rage. Then his expression turned to one of cold hauteur and he slowly rose to his feet. With a curt nod to Sloan, he strode away from the table.

"A pity," Sloan said at length. "I fear Benjamin may never recover from your . . . rejection."

Vivian fluttered her lashes. "You aren't angry with me, are you, Ambrose?"

"Angry?" Sloan repeated in a deep baritone voice. "I couldn't be more delighted, my dear. I've been trying to edge Benjamin out since the night we met. A threesome was simply too—awkward."

"Truly?" Vivian gushed. "You wanted me all for yourself?"

"Yes, indeed," Sloan said triumphantly. "Benjamin's a grand fellow and all that. But shall we say he was an obstacle to my affection for you."

"Holy Hannah!" Vivian appeared enchanted. "You could charm the birds right out of the trees."

"Let us hope so." Sloan grinned, and brushed knees

with her under the table. "I have some rather extraordinary plans in mind for later."

"Naughty man." Vivian smiled suggestively. "You wouldn't take advantage of a girl, would you?"

"Come home with me tonight and find out."

"Ambrose, I wouldn't miss it for the world!"

Vivian laughed and Sloan refilled the glasses. They toasted one another and quaffed the champagne in a gulp. Then he poured again and stared into her eyes with a look of onrushing conquest. She proceeded to drink him under the table.

Vivian possessed an uncanny insight into the male mentality. She knew that some men were strong and others were weak, and she read their minds like an omniscient gypsy witch. Her inner voice told her that Ambrose Sloan was an emotional cripple.

Sloan was lean and muscular, with hawklike features and virile good looks. He was urbane and glib, with a droll sense of humor and a certain sardonic self-assurance. Yet, for all his outward trappings of virility, Vivian sensed he was not secure in his own manhood. Secretly, he was obsessed with the need to please, and an even deeper yearning to be dominated. So he was driven by an overwhelming compulsion to appear the perfect lover, a man who was at once skilled in erotic technique and brute rapine, a conquering, trumpeting stallion who drove women insane with desire.

Apart from reading his mind, Vivian had resorted to an age old stratagem normally used on the weaker sex. The art of seduction, as practiced by randy cocksmen, was nine parts alcohol and one part charm. Not surprisingly, then, Vivian's advantage tonight had been increased many-fold by the quantity of champagne they'd consumed. While she had paced herself, Sloan had swilled with a thirst fueled by lust. He was drunk as a lord.

Earlier, after the Palace closed, Sloan had brought her to his home in Fresno's upper-class residential section. She was at first submissive, allowing herself to be pawed and fondled with kittenish modesty. Then, pretending ardor stoked by his rough caresses, she let him undress her and lead her to a massive four-poster in the bedroom. She lay there now, watching him tear off his own clothes with fumbling haste. He grinned at her like an exultant satyr.

The moment he hopped into bed, Vivian took charge. Avoiding a slobbery kiss, she grabbed him by the ears and forced his head downward. The sudden reversal of roles seemed to fan his passion. Anxious to please, compelled to prove himself, he dutifully went lower and lower. She spread her legs wide and arched her mound upward and he wedged the whole of his head between her thighs. He parted the soft folds of her vulva and his mouth closed over her in a greedy sucking action. His tongue began to probe her crevice, flicking and darting on her sensitive spot with ever faster tempo. The exquisite shock sent needles of fire throughout her body and she was suddenly unable to restrain herself. She hunched forward, forcing herself deeper into his mouth and his tongue penetrated her slippery chalice to the very root. Trapped within the damp convolutions of her body, he wiggled the tip of his tongue and a spark ignited her nerves with an electrifying jolt. She clove tighter to his head, lost in a moment of unbearable rapture, and climaxed in a volcanic eruption that left her dizzy and drained. He lapped her creamy juices like a milk-fed vampire.

Still the aggressor, Vivian abruptly flung her legs over his shoulders and locked him in a scissorhold. Her hand found the hard erect length of him and jacked it back and forth in a rapid whipping motion. Then, opening herself wide with one hand, she slowly rubbed the head of his phallus between the hot, wet lips of her cunt. He groaned deep in his chest, his mouth skinned back to reveal his teeth in a grimace of ecstatic torture. Before he could react, she clamped down with her legs and thrust upward with her buttocks. The impact joined them in perfect union and drove his cock to the depths of her fountainhead. She hung on with her legs, rotating her hips, and pumped him up and down. He shivered, his arms strapped around her thighs, and exploded in a searing rush that snapped his head back in a keening moan. All but paralyzed a moment, he finally shuddered and rolled away as she released her scissorhold. He flopped down beside her, panting heavily, exhausted.

Vivian sighed inwardly. She'd come, by virtue of his tongue, and in the shortest possible time she had forced him to pop his rocks. The physical release was exhilarating, and while she felt slightly soiled, she had to admit she'd enjoyed herself. But the game had only just begun, and now she collected herself for the critical match of wits. For a brief interlude, the combination of champagne and lovemaking made him vulnerable. Flattery was the key to his vanity, and those hidden doubts about his manhood. She deliberately set out to exploit the moment.

"Ummm, that was yummy, Ambrose."

She stretched voluptuously, her breasts round and full. Then she turned, her lips close to his ear, and her hand squeezed his cock with an intimate touch. Her voice was furry velvet.

"What you've got there is the answer to every girl's prayer. You drove me wild, Ambrose."

Sloan gave her a sly and tipsy glance. "Since we're being vulgar about it, you may henceforth address me as 'Ambrose the fucking machine.' I ream any hole to new and unimaginable dimensions."

"Oooo honeybun!" Vivian's eyes twinkled. "I do love a man who's all man. And there's never been another one like yours—not ever!"

"Yes." Sloan's speech was slurred, almost a lisp. "So I've been told before."

"I know!" Vivian laughed a deep, throaty laugh. "All the girls at the Palace talk about you constantly."

"Do they?" Sloan perked up noticeably. "What do they say?"

"Well, for one thing," Vivian said with soft wonder, "any one of them would give her eye teeth to get you in bed. They say a girl's still a virgin till she's been fucked by Ambrose Sloan."

Sloan chortled drunkenly. "How perceptive of them. Anything else?"

"Oh, gobs and gobs!" Vivian marveled. "Especially about your work. They say you're the only lawyer in California with balls enough to take on the Southern Pacific."

"True," Sloan replied loftily. "To tilt at windmills does indeed require a large set of balls."

"Windmills?" Vivian shook her head dumbly. "I dunno about that. But the girls told me how you and some colonel slugged it out toe-to-toe with the railroad. I forget his name."

"McQuade," Sloan grunted. "A major rather than a colonel, and a more pompous ass you'll never hope to meet."

"No kidding?" Vivian looked surprised. "Well, let me tell you, everybody thinks you and him are some team. God, you ought to hear them talk!"

"Team?" Sloan jerked as though a fly had buzzed his ear. "What tommyrot! We're barely on speaking terms. I have no use for a self-professed altruist—damnable hypocrite!"

"Omigosh!" Vivian said, round-eyed. "You mean he's not on the up and up?"

"Shall we say"—Sloan's smile seemed frozen—"Major Thomas McQuade is not all he appears."

Vivian hesitated, chose her words with care. "Well, I sure hope he's not taking those farmers for a ride. Even the sporting crowd's pulling for them. Everybody wants to see the railroad get its ears pinned back."

"I share the sentiment." Sloan hiccupped and covered his mouth. "As for McQuade, I have no faith in the man. I've suspected all along he's playing a game of his own."

"A con game?" Vivian encouraged him. "I don't understand, Ambrose. How would he gain if the farmers lose?"

"How indeed?" Sloan answered dully. "McQuade isn't talking and I've somehow misplaced my crystal ball. Perhaps we'll never know."

Vivian almost laughed out loud. She suddenly saw the whole evening as an immense joke on herself. Earlier, fuming at Tallman for screwing in the line of duty, she'd convinced herself that tit-for-tat was only fair. But now, having seduced Ambrose Sloan, she realized it was an exercise in futility. She'd learned nothing of value and she was still pea-green with jealousy.

A loud snoring sound broke her spell. She looked around and saw that Sloan had drifted off into a sodden sleep. It passed through her mind that she would always remember his tongue with fondness. Yet she nonetheless breathed a sigh of relief.

Once a night in the line of duty was enough.

ELEVEN

Streetlamps flickered like columns of fireflies along Hanford's main street. Tallman stepped from the café, a cigar clamped between his teeth. For a moment, he stood looking at the saloon, attracted by a sudden burst of laughter. Then his eyes rimmed with disgust and he jammed his hands into his pockets. He walked toward the hotel.

Before dawn that morning, he'd returned to Hanford on the night train. Sticking to alleyways, he had made his way to the hotel and entered by the firestairs. There, safely in his room, he'd stowed the bum's costume in his suitcase and caught a couple of hours sleep. Upon awakening, he had bathed and shaved, and donned his regular clothes. He emerged from the hotel in the guise of Alex Fitzhugh.

The balance of the day had been spent asking questions. As the attorney for the Settlers' League, he had an open door anywhere in Hanford. Everyone was aware he'd been retained to tackle the railroad, and their interest proved something more than idle curiosity. Wherever he stopped, the townspeople were concerned about the League's plans; conflict with the Southern Pacific would directly affect the future of the community. By playing on their fears, he'd got them to talk with candor about every aspect of the situation, both past and present. Then he guilefully steered them to the subject of Major Thomas McQuade.

Everyone knew McQuade had journeyed to Bakersfield and they simply assumed Tallman was marking time until the League leader returned. In the course of conversation, he discovered that McQuade's trips were a regular occurrence, generally once a month. He explored that further, but no one attached any particular significance to the trips. Nor were they overly helpful regarding the period McQuade had resided in Bakersfield. As far as he could determine, McQuade's background was a topic of no great interest to anyone. He'd drawn a blank each time the subject was broached.

Still, there was a general consensus among the townspeople. Whether merchant or banker, saloonkeeper or street-corner loafer, all expressed very much the same opinion. Major McQuade had earned their admiration and respect, and none among them doubted his devotion to the Settlers' League. Hanford regarded him as one of its leading citizens.

With oncoming darkness, Tallman had called it quits. What he'd learned wouldn't fill a thimble, and he had uncovered nothing of a damaging nature. He ended the day with the feeling that Hanford had bestowed a sort of sainthood on Thomas McQuade. His every instinct told him the exact opposite was true. Some sinister plot was afoot, and McQuade was the linchpin in the whole affair. Yet, for all his efforts, Tallman's score for the day stood at double-aught zero. He'd taken supper at the café in glum silence.

Brooding on it now, Tallman passed an alleyway separating the hotel from a hardware store. His mind was in a funk, and for one of the few times in his life, he was taken off guard. A shadowy figure suddenly stepped out of the alley and spoke to him.

"Mr. Fitzhugh?"

Tallman reacted on sheer instinct. All in a motion, he spun toward the voice and his hand snaked inside his coat. Then, on the verge of drawing the Colt, something stayed his hand. He peered closer at the figure, still partially hidden in the darkened alley. He saw what appeared to be a man, dressed in trousers and a loose-fitting work jacket. The face was obscured by the floppy brim of a battered stetson.

"Who are you?"

"Three guesses." The voice was soft, faintly mocking. "And the first two don't count."

"Viv?"

"In the flesh."

Tallman took the cigar from his mouth, dumbfounded. "What the hell are you doing here?"

"Waiting for you." Vivian gestured to a horse standing hipshot at the hitch-rack. "Hired myself a nag and rode on down this afternoon. The train seemed a little risky, too open."

"Why?"

Vivian crooked a finger, wiggled it. "Want to join me in the alley? Or maybe you could sneak me into your room."

"No maybe about it."

Tallman moved into the alley and led the way to the rear of the hotel. There they went up the firestairs and entered a door opening onto the second floor hall. A few moments later they were safely in his room. He lit a lamp and turned, inspecting her outfit. His sour look dissolved into a smile.

"Where'd you get the spiffy duds?"

"You like it?" Vivian struck a pose. "Straight off the rack of Fresno's leading pawn shop. I think it hides the merchandise rather well, don't you?"

"Not bad," Tallman acknowledged. "You've got a definite flair for disguise."

"I had a good teacher."

Vivian tossed the stetson aside and stepped into his arms. She kissed him soundly on the mouth, her hands locked behind his head. When she wiggled closer, he uttered a low chuckle and broke her hold. She protested, but he sat her down in a chair and moved to the bed. He stuck the cigar in his mouth and seated himself.

"All right, let's have it," he said firmly. "What happened in Fresno?"

"Some welcome!" Vivian looked hurt. "I blistered my butt getting here and all you want to do is talk shop. Thanks a lot."

"Business first, fun and games later."

"What makes you think anything happened?"

"You don't lurk around in dark alleys for nothing."

"Good point." Vivian nodded, then smiled a little. "Last night I got Ambrose Sloan drunk as a hootowl. For what it's worth, he gave me the lowdown on McQuade."

"Fast work," Tallman said, obviously pleased. "How'd you manage all that in one night?"

Vivian's cheeks colored. "He took me home with him."

"Uh-huh." Tallman puffed smoke and bobbed his head.

"Go on, don't stop there. What convinced him to talk?"

Vivian wrestled with herself for a moment, then shrugged. "I'll give you the same answer you gave me. Ask me no questions and I'll tell you no lies."

Tallman admired the tip of his cigar. "No sacrifice too great when duty calls. Would that about cover it?"

"Like I said," Vivian paused, looked him straight in the eye. "I had a good teacher."

"Touché!" Tallman laughed. "We're even and no harm done. So tell me what you found out?"

"Nothing."

"I thought you said Sloan talked."

"He did and he didn't."

"Try to be more specific."

Vivian briefed him on her evening with Ambrose Sloan. She repeated, almost verbatim, the lawyer's drunken allegations about McQuade. She was careful to note that Sloan possessed no proof and neither had he evidenced any knowledge of McQuade's motives. She skipped the seduction and offered no explanation of how she'd conned Sloan into talking. Her account was straightforward and brisk, very businesslike.

"All in all," she concluded, "it was pretty much a washout. A lot of supposition but no hard facts."

Tallman scratched his jaw thoughtfully. "What was your immediate reaction, Viv? Did you believe him—or not?"

"Well, yes." Vivian blinked with surprise. "I hadn't really stopped to think about it. But looking back, I suppose I did believe him. Why do you ask?"

"I trust your judgment," Tallman said simply. "If you're convinced there's no collusion between McQuade and

Sloan, then we'll lay that theory to rest. Any second thoughts?"

"No," Vivian said calmly. "Ambrose Sloan has nothing but contempt for McQuade. I'm sure of that much, anyway."

"Good girl." Tallman hesitated, considering. "It occurs to me that your night wasn't entirely wasted. Sloan told us a great deal more than meets the eye."

"Oh?" Vivian sounded doubtful. "Such as?"

"For one thing, he confirmed our own suspicions. He branded McQuade a hypocrite and accused him of playing an underhanded game. Considering that he's worked with McQuade, it's a telling argument. I tend to buy it."

"So do I," Vivian conceded. "What else?"

Tallman flicked the ash off his cigar. "I'm intrigued by a comment Sloan made. The one about 'tilting at windmills.' In so many words, he was saying the fight with the Southern Pacific was hopeless from the outset. I think it's safe to conclude he probably told McQuade the same thing. See my point?"

"Of course!" Vivian stiffened, sat erect. "If McQuade knew that from the beginning, then he's just been stringing the farmers along. All his fire and brimstone preaching was a lie from start to finish. No wonder Sloan called him a hypocrite!"

"Exactly," Tallman affirmed. "So we come again to the crux of the matter—McQuade's motive."

Vivian eyed him quizzically. "Why do I get the feeling you know something I don't?"

Tallman laughed a short, mirthless laugh. "The Major

took a little sojourn down to Bakersfield yesterday. I slipped into a disguise of my own . . . and tailed him."

Vivian laughed and clapped her hands together like an exuberant child. "So tell me what happened. Where'd he lead you?"

"To the Kern County Land and Development Company."

"The what?"

"Suppose we back up and let me explain."

Tallman covered his surveillance of McQuade quickly and without elaboration. His remarks centered mostly on McQuade's determined effort to move unobserved through downtown Bakersfield. The League leader's secretive manner, he noted, spoke for itself. There was something very fishy about the visit to the Kern County Land and Development Company.

"In short," he observed, "a man with legitimate business doesn't worry about a tail. So we have to ask ourselves the obvious question. Why was McQuade trying to hide his tracks?"

"I'll hazard a guess," Vivian said cautiously. "Your investigation today established that he makes these trips once a month. Wouldn't it follow that his dealings with the land company began before he moved to Hanford?"

"Very good!" Tallman nodded gravely. "And by following that line of reasoning, we come to the heart of the matter. Is it possible the land company *sent* McQuade to Hanford?"

"Wait a minute!" Vivian's gaze sharpened. "Are you saying he was sent here to create trouble? I suppose it's possible, but where's the logic? What value would the farms here have to a land company in Bakersfield? The Southern Pacific already holds prior claim—by court order."

"Quite right," Tallman said, almost dreamily. "Which leads me to believe the farmers here are merely pawns in a larger game. Something no one—not even the railroad— would suspect."

Vivian considered the thought. "You leapfrogged way too far for me. What larger game?"

Tallman threw up his hands and rolled his eyes. "We won't know that until we've done some spade work on the land company. So we're going to shift the operation to Bakersfield."

"Won't that tip our hand to McQuade?"

Quickly, Tallman outlined the plan he'd formulated. The time factor was critical, and he readily admitted there was no margin for error. Vivian listened, thoroughly engrossed by the audacity of the scheme. When he finished, there was a devilish glint in her eye. She laughed and tossed her head.

"I love it! How fast do we move?"

"Immediately," Tallman said briskly. "You ride on back to Fresno—"

"Tonight?" Vivian wailed. "Have a heart, lover. All work and no play makes Viv a dull girl."

"You'll live," Tallman said with a wry chuckle. "Keep it warm till we get to Bakersfield. We'll make up for lost time then."

Tallman stood and crossed the room. He lifted her out of her chair, embracing her with a crushing bear hug and a long kiss. Then he jammed her stetson on her head and hustled her out the door. The hallway was deserted and he led her swiftly down the rear firestairs. She was still sulking as they moved along the darkened alley. On the street, they walked straight to the hitch-rack. Vivian's horse snorted and eyed them warily.

"Fitzhugh!"

A rough shout stopped them cold. Tallman saw Floyd Hull, the farmer he'd whipped, step off the boardwalk fronting the saloon. Hull lurched toward them, clearly tanked to the gills and spoiling for trouble. Tallman scanned the street and spotted no one else about. He muttered a warning to Vivian and she tugged her hat lower. Then Hull halted before them with a look of drunken rage.

"Awright, put your dukes up, hotshot! I'm gonna clean your plow!"

"You're crocked," Tallman said reasonably. "Go sleep it off and try me when you're sober."

"Son of a bitch!" Hull snarled. "I ain't waitin' no longer. You're due to get your ashes hauled and tonight's the night."

"Tell you what," Tallman said, stalling him. "Let me see my friend off and then we'll talk about it. Fair enough?"

Hull laughed a wild, braying laugh. "Whyn't I just stomp the both of you? C'mon, let 'er rip, shorty!"

Hull shoved Vivian and she slammed up against the horse. Her hat was dislodged and auburn curls spilled down over her forehead. In the glow of the streetlamp, her features were distinct, her beauty all too apparent. She tried to recover, but Hull was gawking at her now. His expression was one of stupid disbelief.

"Gawddamn, you ain't no—"

Tallman's fist lashed out in a shadowy blur. The blow caught Hull flush on the jaw and his knees buckled. Tallman spun him around and delivered a short, chopping right cross to the chin. Hull staggered backwards and went down on the seat of his pants in the alleyway. He shook off the effect of the punch, eyes glazed with hatred, and let go a murderous oath. His hand dipped inside his coat and came out with a bulldog revolver.

Vivian shot him. Her tiny derringer was extended arm's length and the sharp report split the night. Hull's left eye disappeared, almost as though he had winked. The slug blew out the back of his skull in a misty halo of brains and bone matter. His bowels voided in death and he slumped to the ground without a sound. His hand still clutched the revolver.

Without a word, Tallman lifted her bodily and hoisted her into the saddle. Vivian tucked the derringer into her coat pocket as he handed her the reins and backed the horse into the street. Stepping aside, he swatted the horse across the rump and Vivian bent low over the saddlehorn. She thundered northward out of town as a knot of men burst through the saloon door. Tallman gestured violently at the fleeing horse and rider. Then he turned toward the men with a leather-lunged cry of alarm.

"After him! Somebody stop him! He murdered Floyd Hull!"

TWELVE

A crowd of townspeople stood bunched together outside the marshal's office. Word of the killing had spread like wildfire, and as dawn lighted the horizon the crowd steadily increased in size. There was a ghoulish aspect to their vigil, mingled with dark mutterings. No official announcement had yet cleared Alex Fitzhugh of murder.

The door of the jailhouse was locked and barred. Marshal Daniel Garland stood with his hands clasped behind his back. He was a man of immense girth, with sad eyes and graying hair and a soup-strainer mustache. A Colt Peacemaker was bucked on his hip, cinched tight under a belly that spilled over his gunbelt. He was staring out the window with a troubled expression, his gaze fixed on the crowd.

Tallman was seated in a chair before the desk. His Colt 41 was centered perfectly on the desktop, and beside it five cartridges were aligned like soldiers on parade. Last night, with Floyd Hull not yet cold, the marshal had been summoned to the scene of the shooting. After hearing Tallman's story, he'd ordered the body removed by the undertaker. Then he had disarmed Tallman and marched him off to the city jail.

For the next hour or so, the marshal had questioned the saloon crowd. All of them substantiated that a rider had indeed flogged his horse out of town. Yet no one had actually witnessed the shooting, which left only Tallman's word as to who had fired the fatal shot. Finally, the marshal had shooed everyone out and barred the door. He'd then informed Tallman that no formal charges would be pressed. In the next breath, he had allowed that a night spent in protective custody would benefit all concerned. The dead man had friends in town, and it took only a few hotheads to turn a crowd into an ugly mob. Daniel Garland wanted no part of a lynching bee.

For his part, Tallman considered the precaution unnecessary. His story was airtight—particularly with no eyewitnesses—and the physical evidence supported his version of the shooting. So he smoked quietly and stared off into some thoughtful distance. His mind was on Vivian, and their plan to shift the investigation to Bakersfield. By now she was in Fresno, already engaged in putting together her new disguise. She would expect him there by early evening, which was when they'd arranged to meet at the train depot. But he still had things to do and people to see before he could depart Hanford. High on the list was a credible cover story for Major McQuade. He decided it was time to part company with the marshal.

"How much longer do you plan on holding me?"

Garland turned from the window. "What's your rush?"

"No rush," Tallman replied with a vague wave of his

hand. "But as you have no doubt noted . . . it's daylight."

"What I note," Garland said grimly, "is that crowd outside. It's not gettin' any smaller."

"Perhaps they're waiting for you to make some sort of announcement."

"Got any suggestions?"

"You might inform them I've been cleared."

"Then what?"

"Then you release me and we all get on with our business. Major McQuade's due back in town on the noon train, and it's important I meet with him."

"That a fact?" Garland motioned out the window. "Some folks in that crowd might try to stop you. Maybe you wouldn't never make your meeting."

"I'll take my chances," Tallman said coolly. "Assuming, of course, you're willing to return my gun."

"One dead man's enough. I'd sooner let things lay a while longer."

"And if I insist?"

"Don't," Garland said stolidly. "Just hold your water till I say otherwise. The noon train's generally late anyway."

Tallman's protest was cut short. There was a buzz of excitement outside and Garland turned to the window. His features screwed up in a tight scowl and he cursed under his breath. A moment later three hard raps sounded at the door.

"We got new trouble," Garland mumbled. "Our no-account sheriff just dealt himself a hand."

"What's the problem?"

"Isaac Wilcox and me don't exactly see eye-to-eye. He's a flunky for the Southern Pacific."

"No joke?"

"Gospel fact," Garland warned, moving toward the door. "Watch your step. He's tricky as they come."

"I certainly will, Marshal."

Tallman's naiveté was all pretense. He recalled the meeting with Otis Blackburn, general superintendent of the Southern Pacific. At the time, Blackburn had bluntly stated that the sheriff was a political lackey for the railroad. Apparently the Southern Pacific owned most of the courthouse crowd in Kings County. The killing of Floyd Hull suddenly took on a new and threatening dimension. Tallman cautioned himself to play it close to the vest.

Garland unbarred the door and stepped aside. Sheriff Isaac Wilcox stormed into the office with a look of towering wrath. He whirled around as Garland once more barred the door. His tone was hard, cutting.

"You got some gall, Garland!"

"Don't work yourself into a swivet, Sheriff."

"I got reason! There was a killing last night and I only heard about it ten minutes ago. How d'you explain that?"

"Happened in town," Garland said tonelessly. "Not your bailiwick."

"Like hell!" Wilcox roared. "Murder's a capital offense. That makes it county business—*my* business."

"Not unless somebody prefers charges."

Garland crossed the room and took a seat behind his desk. The chair creaked ominously under his weight and he leaned back with his hands folded over his belly. Then he nodded toward Tallman.

"This here's Alex Fitzhugh. He's the only witness to

the shooting and his story suits me just fine. I don't see no reason to hold him."

"I'll decide that!" Wilcox snapped. "But not till I've heard it firsthand for myself."

Tallman steeled himself for a grilling. The sheriff clearly had no idea he was a Pinkerton, working undercover for the railroad. His association with the Settlers' League, insofar as Wilcox was concerned, immediately placed him in the enemy camp. He found a certain irony in the situation.

Wilcox perched on the edge of the desk. He put his hands on his knees and gave Tallman a straight hard look. His tone was curt and inquisitorial.

"You're the new lawyer for the Settlers' League?"

"Quite so, Sheriff."

"I understand you hit town less'n a week ago?"

"Correct."

"Fast operator, aren't you?" Wilcox's brow furrowed. "Or maybe McQuade imported you from somewheres?"

"No," Tallman said with a blank stare. "But, then, that's hardly germane to the matter at hand. Wouldn't you agree, Sheriff?"

"Don't get smart!" Wilcox paused, and the timbre of his voice changed. "Wasn't Floyd Hull a member of the League?"

"I fail to see the connection."

"You and Hull had a run-in, didn't you?"

"A slight altercation." Tallman regarded him evenly. "Nothing of consequence."

"Oh, no?" Wilcox said scornfully. "I heard you whaled the shit outta him."

"Then I presume you also heard it was a case of self-defense. Hull was drunk and picked a fight."

"Was he drunk last night?"

Tallman sensed a trap. "Not drunk, but not sober either. He was navigating at about half-speed."

"Do tell?" Wilcox said with a clenched smile. "I stopped off at the saloon on my way over here. The barkeep says Hull was drunker'n a fiddler's bitch. How d'you explain that?"

"I wouldn't try." Tallman puffed his cigar and blew a perfect smoke ring toward the ceiling. "Hull was coherent and operating under his own faculties. In barroom vernacular, he was neither sloshed nor ossified."

"He was drunk enough though, wasn't he?"

"Your meaning eludes me, Sheriff."

"The hell it does. Floyd Hull had a reputation for never forgetting an insult. He braced you last night and tried to even the score. Do you deny it?"

"You aren't serious," Tallman said with a leer of disbelief. "Are you actually implying that I shot Hull?"

"If not you"—Wilcox squinted querulously—"then who?"

"I really couldn't say." A smile shadowed Tallman's lips. "The man who killed him was a total stranger."

"Why would a stranger shoot him?"

"The man accosted me on the street and was in the process of robbing me at gunpoint. Hull appeared out of the alley and attempted to intervene. The robber shot him dead, then jumped on a horse and galloped away. I was lucky to escape with my life."

"Christ on a crutch!" Wilcox's voice rose suddenly. "Are you telling me Floyd Hull got himself killed trying to rescue you from a robber?"

"Precisely," Tallman said with dungeon calm. "In the end, he displayed pure and unalloyed true grit. He deserves a medal."

"Hogshit!" Wilcox exploded. "You're lying through your teeth!"

"No, he's not," Garland interjected. "I disarmed him right after the shooting. His gun was fully loaded and it hadn't been fired. Have a look for yourself."

Wilcox took the Colt off the desk. He smelled the muzzle and flicked a glance at the five unfired cartridges. Then he thumbed the hammer and let off the trigger. His eyes swung back to Tallman.

"A hair-trigger," he said accusingly. "And it's been honed by a professional. Why would a lawyer carry a gun like that?"

"Why not?" Tallman smiled vacantly. "We live in a violent world, Sheriff. A wise man arms himself with only the very best."

Wilcox's gaze went stony. "If you're so experienced, why'd you let the robber get away? You could've blasted him to ribbons while he was busy killin' Hull."

"It all happened so fast," Tallman said earnestly. "Besides, I haven't fired a gun in anger since the war. I'm afraid I've lost the killer instinct."

"Balls," Wilcox said with a lightning frown. "You've got guilt written all over you."

"Stop badgering him," Garland leaned forward, elbows

on the desk. "He's clean and we both know it. So just leave it be."

"You're one to talk." Wilcox glared owlishly. "Why the hell didn't you raise a posse and go after this phantom robber?"

"Too dark to track," Garland bristled. "And he wasn't no phantom. A dozen men saw him ride out of town."

"Maybe so," Wilcox replied angrily. "But that doesn't excuse dereliction of duty. You should've squeezed your lardass into a saddle and gave it a try."

"That's enough!" Garland slammed a meaty fist into the desktop. "Only reason you're here is because Fitzhugh works for the League, and I've had it. I'd advise you to waltz out the same way you come in."

Wilcox's jawline tightened. "You tryin' to threaten me?"

"I'll do more'n that," Garland said with cold menace. "You make tracks or I'll spread the word you've been ordered to persecute the League's lawyer. Folks would tend to believe it, too. Especially since they know you hocked your soul to the Southern Pacific."

"No truth to it!" Wilcox's eyes blazed. "I uphold the law fair and square. You got no call to say otherwise."

"Quit squawkin'," Garland said, motioning toward the door. "On your way out, tell the crowd you've questioned Fitzhugh and you're satisfied he's in the clear. Don't forget or I'm liable to give 'em a stemwinder about you and the railroad."

Wilcox suddenly looked uncomfortable. He tossed the Colt on the desk with a vicious curse and rose to his feet. Then he stalked across the room and let himself out. The door rattled on its hinges.

Tallman burst out laughing. "I owe you one, Marshal. You chopped his legs off at the knees."

"Forget it," Garland said crisply. "That was between Wilcox and me. Had nothin' to do with you."

"All the same, I'm in your debt."

"Everybody owes somebody, Mr. Fitzhugh. I reckon it's what makes the world go 'round."

"A loud amen to that, Marshal!"

The noontime regulars jammed the bar. Apart from spirits, a free lunch counter always attracted a crowd. The atmosphere today was convivial but subdued.

Tallman and Major McQuade were seated at one of the rear tables. After meeting the noon train, Tallman had explained the events of last night. McQuade, who seemed somewhat preoccupied, had accepted his version of the killing. Some sixth sense told Tallman that McQuade's trip had not gone well. The thought merely reinforced the urgency of shifting the investigation to Bakersfield. Yet now, sipping whiskey, Tallman was wary of the plunge. He decided to test the water.

"I was wondering," he ventured, "if you know the date the government passed land title to the Southern Pacific. By any chance was it brought out in court?"

McQuade shook his head. "What's so important about the date?"

"I suspect it would coincide almost exactly with the date the railroad ordered your people to vacate their farms."

"Even so, what would that get us?"

"Perhaps a reversal in the Supreme Court. It would

represent prima facie evidence that the Southern Pacific allowed you to go on improving the land when all the while they meant to dispossess you."

McQuade examined the notion. "I think it's got possibilities, Alex."

"Indeed it does," Tallman said confidently. "You asked me to work out a plan and that's the first step. Somewhere in the state capital we'll find a record of the transfer. So I'll have to travel to Sacramento to verify the date."

"When will you leave?"

"Today," Tallman informed him. "When I finish there, I want to nose around San Francisco a bit. Perhaps I can turn up a link between the railroad and the district court judge. If so, we could charge the Southern Pacific with conspiracy and call for a grand jury investigation. Win or lose, we'd put them on the defensive."

"Sounds like a longshot to me."

"Nothing ventured, nothing gained," Tallman said with a laugh. "You wanted action and I aim to please."

McQuade gave him an odd, steadfast look. "Don't show the bastards any mercy, Alex. Get in there and crack heads!"

Tallman smiled into his whiskey. "I'll do my damnedest, Major."

"How long will you be gone?"

"A week, more or less."

"Bring me Leland Stanford's head on a platter!"

"Hell, I'll even try for an apple in his mouth!"

Some while later, Tallman boarded the afternoon train.

Up the line, Vivian waited for him in Fresno. By nightfall, they would reverse course and be on their way to Bakersfield. Then, at last, the game would begin in earnest.

A variation on the Big Con.

THIRTEEN

The courthouse clock tolled the hour. On the stroke of three, a hansom cab crossed the square in downtown Bakersfield. The driver reined to a halt in front of a three-story brick hotel, jumped down to the curb and opened the door.

As Tallman stepped out of the cab his gaze lingered briefly on the deserted square, lighted by a waning moon and sparkling streetlamps. Then he turned and offered his hand to Vivian. She sniffed, ignoring his hand, and allowed the driver to assist her down. Tallman shrugged and pulled out his wallet.

"How much do we owe you, driver?"

"I will pay my own fare, thank you!"

Vivian unsnapped her purse and handed the driver five dollars. She indicated no change was necessary and flounced away. The generous tip was in keeping with her regal manner and her stylish attire. She wore a tailored suit, navy blue serge with a pleated skirt and a jacket trimmed with dark gray bone buttons. Her white shirt-waist had fluffy ruffles at the throat and an exquisite array of feathers decorated her hat. She looked every inch a woman of breeding and expensive tastes.

The driver scrambled to collect her luggage and hatbox from the top of the cab. Without a backward glance, Vivian swept into the hotel like visiting royalty. She was trailed by the driver and Tallman, who carried his own rather shop-worn carpetbag. The click of her heels on the marble floor echoed throughout the dimly lit lobby. A sleepy night clerk bounded to his feet behind the desk and stared wide-eyed at the fashionably dressed lady and her entourage. Vivian nodded with a condescending smile.

"Mrs. Varina Thorn," she announced grandly. "I wish to engage a suite."

"Yes, ma'am!" The clerk darted a look at Tallman. "How long will you and Mr. Thorn be with us?"

"This *gentleman*," Vivian said with withering sarcasm, "is *not* Mr. Thorn. We happened to arrive on the same train, and at this hour of the morning, there was only one cab available. I regret to say we were forced to share it."

Tallman stepped forward. "The name's Edmund Scott. A plain old room will do just fine for me." He cut his eyes at Vivian and gave the clerk a slow wink. "Not that I wouldn't prefer the suite."

"Now really!" Vivian thrust her nose into the air. "I have tolerated your boorish humor long enough. Please be so kind as to wait your turn!"

The clerk looked embarrassed and the cab driver hastily retreated out the door. Tallman grinned and moved aside while Vivian signed the register. A porter was summoned from a back room and the clerk handed him a key.

"Show Mrs. Thorn to suite three-oh-nine."

Vivian walked straight to the elevator. The porter hefted her luggage and hurried along behind. A moment later the cage door closed and Vivian stared icily into space as the elevator disappeared from view. The clerk watched after her in bemused silence. Tallman scribbled his cover name in the ledger.

"No luck tonight," he said, chuckling softly. "Thought I had myself a live one and then she turned snooty on me. Guess there's no figuring women."

The clerk produced a key without comment. "You're on the second floor, Mr. Scott. Would you care to wait for the elevator?"

"No, thanks. I'll manage on my own."

Tallman crossed the lobby and went up a broad staircase. On the second floor, he found his room and dropped off the carpetbag. Then he took the stairs to the third floor and paused, surveying the hallway. The porter was nowhere in sight and he walked rapidly to the door of suite 309. He knocked once.

Vivian let him in and closed the door. She twisted the key, then turned with a dazzling smile. "Not bad, huh? How'd you like my Lady Astor act?"

Tallman thought it had gone very well indeed. Early that evening, he'd stepped off the train in Fresno and found Vivian waiting. Within the hour, they had boarded the southbound, headed for Bakersfield. The ruse was perfectly coordinated, and neither of them had left any loose ends. Vivian would simply disappear from Fresno, written off by Ambrose Sloan and the theater owner as another vagabond saloon girl. As for Tallman, a week or so would pass before McQuade expected him back in

Hanford. Thus far, everything had come off according to schedule and he anticipated no problems. Their entrance into the hotel had set the stage for the next phase of the operation.

"Well, Lady Astor," he said lightly, "we're off and running. All you have to do now is vamp Harlan Ordway."

"I'll worry about him tomorrow."

Vivian got a sexy look in her eyes. He laughed and scooped her up in his arms and carried her to bed. Soon they were naked, and she shed her ladylike airs with the blue serge suit. All thought of tomorrow was suspended the moment they joined.

Neither of them heard the courthouse clock strike four.

Tallman emerged from the hotel around eleven. A bright morning sun blazed down on the square and the sidewalks were crowded with shoppers. He crossed the street and mounted the steps to the courthouse. Inside, he proceeded along a central corridor to the county clerk's office. He passed himself off as a land speculator and slipped the county clerk a swift fifty dollars. Several minutes later he was seated in the storage room and spread out before him was a musty ledger. He began reading.

The ledger was a record of all land sales in Kern County over the past year. Tallman reasoned that the court battle with the Southern Pacific had begun last year, and therefore any connection to Harlan Ordway's land company would have occurred within the same time span. He had no idea what form the connection might take; whether or not it even existed was a matter of pure conjecture. Yet he was no great believer in coincidence, and he was spurred on by the thought of McQuade's trip to Bakersfield. His search now was for the connecting thread.

Line by line, Tallman went through the ledger. He paused only when he found an entry dealing with the Kern County Land & Development Company and then jotted down the particulars of every purchase and sale on a notepad. The process was tedious and time consuming, for recorded there were location and sales price, title search and survey lines, and the date of transfer. By the number of entries, it soon became obvious that Ordway's company monopolized land sales in Kern County. The amount of money involved was staggering, totaling upwards of two million dollars in one year alone. Harlan Ordway was clearly no piker.

Whatever Tallman expected to find, he was somewhat puzzled by what he finally uncovered. A large map of Kern County was tacked to the storage room wall. By comparing entries in the ledger to grids on the map, he was able to determine the exact location of each purchase and sale. The transactions covered the compass, spread throughout the whole of Kern County. Ever so slowly, however, a pattern began to take shape. Ordway's company had bought a great deal of land and resold it for a handsome profit. Yet, as verified by the transfer dates, abutting parcels of land had been systematically purchased along a strip located in the southeastern quadrant of the county. And once purchased, none of these parcels had been resold. The company now owned a corridor of land, plainly obvious on the map, stretching southeastward on a beeline from Bakersfield. The land was in the opposite direction from Los

Angeles and other populous areas, and clearly had no connection with the Southern Pacific railway line. All of which left Tallman scratching his head.

Why would Harlan Ordway methodically buy and hold land running due southeast? A strip of land that seemingly went nowhere.

On the stroke of one, Vivian strolled out of the hotel. She wore an ivory gown of tucked linen, with vermillion lace-velvet trim across the bodice and shoulders. She carried a dainty parasol and atop her head was a bowed straw hat ablaze with roses. She looked ravishing.

Heads craned as she snapped open her parasol and walked toward the northeast corner of the square. Several men tipped their hats and women stared daggers as she passed by at a leisurely pace. Oblivious to it all, she turned the corner onto a side street. Halfway down the block she paused and made a small production of closing her parasol. Then she entered the Kern County Land & Development Company.

In the outer office, a girl seated at a reception desk gave her an envious once-over. Vivian tucked the parasol under her arm and smiled graciously.

"Good afternoon. I would like to speak with Mr. Harlan Ordway."

"May I tell him who's calling?"

"Mrs. Varina Thorn."

"One moment."

The girl rapped lightly on the door of a private office and entered. A few seconds passed, then the door opened and she reappeared. She stood aside and gestured with a sweeping motion.

"Won't you come this way, Mrs. Thorn?"

Harlan Ordway rose from behind his desk as Vivian moved through the door. He was handsome, though somewhat heavyset, with prominent cheekbones and a mane of dark hair. Vivian had the immediate impression of a man with hard eyes and a winning smile, someone at once impenetrable and cunning. He offered her a chair and resumed his seat.

"How may I help you, Mrs. Thorn?"

Vivian placed her hands demurely in her lap, knees together. "I wish to make some investments, Mr. Ordway. I understand your firm deals exclusively in land."

"I see." Ordway's voice was bland as butter. "Will it be a coventure . . . with Mr. Thorn?"

"I fear not," Vivian said with a melancholy smile. "I am recently widowed, Mr. Ordway. My husband passed away early last month."

"A shame," Ordway intoned. "Allow me to offer my condolences."

"You're very kind."

Ordway modestly dismissed it with a wave of his hand. "Are you a resident of Kern County, Mrs. Thorn?

"Not yet," Vivian remarked. "However, I plan to move here after settling my affairs in San Francisco."

"Do you?" Ordway's smile was cryptic. "May I ask why you chose Bakersfield?"

"San Francisco is too—" Vivian lifted one hand in a fluttering gesture. "Oh, how shall I say it? San Francisco is too fast, Mr. Ordway. A widow finds herself at the mercy of unscrupulous charlatans. I prefer to invest in a more bucolic atmosphere."

"Very wise." Ordway fixed her with an eloquent look. "What size investment were you considering?"

"To start," Vivian said matter-of-factly, "I think something on the order of fifty thousand dollars. Depending on the return, I might consider doubling that at some later time."

"A substantial sum!" Ordway beamed a fraudulent smile. "I daresay Mr. Thorn left a sizable estate?"

"Roger was a dear, sweet man." Vivian smiled disarmingly. "Of course, a woman in my position must exercise caution. I wouldn't dream of investing without first inspecting the land. Please don't be offended, Mr. Ordway. It's simply that I fell so vulnerable . . . without Roger."

Ordway wasn't at all offended. "I commend your caution, Mrs. Thorn. In fact, I will personally attend to your investment program myself. Suppose we have a look at some land parcels tomorrow. Would that be convenient?"

"Tomorrow would be perfect, Mr. Ordway."

"Excellent!" Ordway's gaze turned bold, openly suggestive. "Perhaps you would have dinner with me tonight, Mrs. Thorn? I'd be very pleased to show you around our fair city."

"I . . ." Vivian hesitated, her eyes flirtatious. "Ask me another time, Mr. Ordway. After we're better . . . acquainted."

"I'll do that very thing!"

"Until tomorrow, then." Vivian stood. "Shall we say ten-ish or so? I'm never at my best early in the morning."

"Consider me at your service—day or night."

Ordway escorted her to the door. Vivian wig-wagged her hips as she crossed the outer office and stepped outside. On the street, she opened her parasol and turned uptown. She was laughing inwardly, delighted with her performance. It was like old times, only better.

Harlan Ordway was all chump and she'd conned him cross-eyed.

Later, in Vivian's suite, they swapped information. Tallman outlined what he'd unearthed at the courthouse and she reenacted the scene with Ordway. After some reflection, Tallman decided to revise the plan. While she kept Ordway occupied, he would investigate the strip of land southeast of town. When time allowed, he would also shadow Ordway and see where that led. One way or another, they were certain to establish the connection to the Southern Pacific. His conviction was stronger than ever that the link existed.

"Sounds good," Vivian said, when he'd finished talking. "So when do I get my reward?"

"What reward?"

"Well, honestly, lover!" Vivian gave him a sassy grin. "I'm not doing this for the money, or for the greater glory of the Pinkerton Agency. Not on your tintype!"

"What'd you have in mind?"

"In a word"—Vivian eyed him with a hungry look—"*you.*"

Tallman stripped her on the spot. Then she lay on the sofa and watched while he shucked his clothes. A pinpoint of fire danced in her eyes as he stepped out of his shorts and his shaft protruded outward like a battering ram. She reached for it, her mouth opened wide, but he caught her wrist and turned her onto her stomach. She quickly positioned herself on the sofa, her arms on the backrest and her knees planted on the cushion. She presented her rump to him and looked over her shoulder. His hand went between her legs and he found her already wet and warm. He slowly caressed the soft, moist nub within the curly swell of her mound. Her head sagged sideways and her breathing quickened.

Holding her hips, he spread her thighs wide apart and drove his cock into her with a swift, stabbing thrust. Her eyes popped open and her head arched back and she emitted a keening wail from her throat. For a moment, the whole of his rod sunk deep inside her, their bodies were fused together, groin to buttocks. Then he leaned forward, moved his hands up the supple curve of her belly and took hold of her full, satiny breasts. He humped, pulling out and plunging in, massaging her nipples as his thrusts gained speed. Her hips moved with instinctual harmony, pumping backwards and forwards, timed with perfect rhythm to the beat of his stroke. He waited until her spine stiffened and her mouth hung open, and then, with all the power of his hard-muscled frame, he rammed inward and drove her across the threshold. His manhood throbbed and quivered and exploded with sharp, jolting eruptions. Her mouth opened in a mindless, shuddering cry.

FOURTEEN

Mr. Wexler?"

"Yes."

"Edmund Scott." Tallman extended his hand. "I'd appreciate some advice—on investments."

"By all means."

Jonathon Wexler was on the sundown side of fifty, overweight and balding and parsimonious by nature. As president of the First National Bank he had few equals in the Bakersfield power structure. He was pleasant, but quietly arrogant, and no one called him John. His office, which was done in lush leather and darkly paneled wood, bespoke his position in the business community. He motioned Tallman to a wingback armchair.

"How may I be of service, Mr. Scott?"

"I've inquired around," Tallman said, lighting a long cigar. "I'm told you're the man who knows everything about anything in Bakersfield."

"Hardly that," Wexler said with a smug look. "People tend to overrate the attributes of a banker."

"You're too modest, Mr. Wexler."

"Not at all, Mr. Scott. In my own small way, I merely serve the public interest. I believe you mentioned investments?"

Tallman's manner was one of bluff assurance. Yet, with some finesse, he was playing on Wexler's high-and-mighty self-importance. He leaned forward now with a conspiratorial grin.

"I trust our conversation will be treated with the utmost confidence."

"A banker," Wexler said pompously, "approaches his work somewhat like a priest. Anything you say will never leave this office."

"Splendid," Tallman said heartily. "Were my plans known, I fear it would drive prices straight through the roof."

Wexler scrutinized him closely. "Am I to assume you're a speculator, Mr. Scott?"

"I prefer to think of myself as an entrepreneur. When opportunity knocks, I sometimes reply with venture capital."

"Uh-huh." Wexler looked interested. "May I ask what you consider venture capital?"

"A quarter of a million, perhaps more."

Wexler coughed, clearly surprised. "Not a trifling sum, Mr. Scott. What attracted you to Bakersfield?"

"I'm from Nevada," Tallman explained, "where I've prospered in real estate and mining and other enterprises. But now I want to diversify into other areas. Something with the potential of unusually high short-term yields."

"And you believe Bakersfield offers such potential?"

"Oh, my, yes!" Tallman nodded soberly. "I've traveled

the San Joaquin Valley from north to south and Bakers-field strikes me as the town of the future. The diversity I seek is apparent everywhere, Mr. Wexler."

"A shrewd observation," Wexler said unctuously. "What type of investments were you considering?"

"There's where I need advice." Tallman paused, blew a plume of smoke into the air. "I've looked at several mining operations, both silver and borax. Which would you recommend as the most profitable?"

"For the short term, I would definitely suggest silver."

"Good," Tallman said, pleased. "That confirms my own estimate. Now, with diversity in mind, I'm also interested in a land venture. Kern County has a thriving citrus industry, and that's one possibility. But I'm not averse to speculation on raw land. Which seems to you the better prospect?"

"No question," Wexler said positively. "Buy raw land and turn it over for a quick profit! Then reinvest—buy and sell—and you won't go wrong. We're in the midst of an agricultural boom."

"Where would I look for prime farm land?"

"Practically anywhere," Wexler replied. "Although you might do well to avoid the southeast part of the county. It's somewhat arid, not too much in the way of natural irrigation. Otherwise, you'll find prime land in all directions."

Tallman studied his cigar, thoughtful. "I'll need someone to represent me in the land transactions. Who would you recommend as an agent?"

"Harlan Ordway," Wexler said without hesitation. "He owns the largest land company in Kern County."

"I take it he's dependable . . . reliable?"

"Oh, absolutely!" Wexler assured him. "I'd trust Harlan Ordway with my last nickel. He's a man of spotless integrity. None better."

"How long has he been in business?"

"Since day one." Wexler chortled. "Long before Bakersfield was incorporated as a town."

Tallman saw no reason to probe further. "I'll have my bank forward a letter of credit for a quarter million. Once you have it on deposit, we can go from there."

"You intend to move quickly, then?"

"With prudent speed," Tallman said, climbing to his feet. "I appreciate the advice, Mr. Wexler. You've been a great help."

"A privilege Mr. Scott." Wexler shook hands warmly. "We're always at your service."

"Good day."

On the street, Tallman crossed the square and walked toward the hotel. For all his guile, he'd conned the banker out of little information. This was his third day in Bakersfield, and he was in a foul mood. He felt he was getting nowhere fast.

The day before he'd hired a horse and ridden southeast out of town. From the map in the county clerk's office, he remembered the topography and the general lay of the land. By dead reckoning, he was able to locate those parcels owned by the Kern County Land & Development Company. He had followed the strip of land for some ten miles, and then stopped, completely baffled. The terrain was dusty and dry; as farmland, it was, for the immediate future, practically worthless. He'd returned to town with lots of questions, and no answers.

Today, he had concentrated his efforts on the townspeople. He'd toured several saloons and gaming dens, passing himself off as a Johnny-come-lately land speculator. By buying drinks, and asking leading questions, he had inevitably worked the subject around to Harlan Ordway. Over the course of the day, he had compiled a fairly detailed dossier. Ordway was one of Bakersfield's original founders, and a widely respected civic leader. He was considered honest to a fault and known to be a devoted family man. While he played around occasionally, his affairs were not looked upon as a vice. He was apparently without blemish or disreputable habits.

Tallman's last stop of the day had been the bank. He'd learned nothing he hadn't already known; but one remark still stuck in his mind. Wexler had discouraged him from investing in the southeastern section of the county. All of which compounded the central questions. Why would Harlan Ordway buy up mile upon mile of valueless land? It beggared explanation, and led to yet another imponderable. How was it linked to the Southern Pacific?

Thoroughly perplexed, Tallman entered the hotel and slowly climbed the stairs. On the third floor, Vivian admitted him to her suite. For the past two days she'd toured a good part of Kern County, looking at parcels of land. Her guide was Harlan Ordway, and the experience was quickly exhausting her patience. She was in a peevish mood.

"Honest to God!" she said, smiling wanly. "A buggy ride with him isn't one you're likely to forget."

"According to the locals," Tallman remarked, "he's an upstanding Christian gentleman."

"Oh, he's upstanding all right." Vivian laughed and

wagged her head. "The bastard's got a hard-on that stands up like a flag pole. He has to sit on it to hide it."

"Got him all hot and bothered, do you?"

"What else?" Vivian's eyes flashed with fierce pride. "You told me to put the whammy on him, and I've done just that. He's drooling."

Tallman's expression turned somber, somehow pensive. "Wish to Christ I had something to report. So far I've come up empty-handed . . . nothing."

"C'mon now!" Vivian arched one eyebrow in question. "Haven't you got a clue? Maybe an itty-bitty hint? I need encouragement."

"Only what I told you," Tallman said in a musing voice. "We know he bought worthless land, but we don't know why. I can't even hazard a guess."

"Well, do something." Vivian looked worried. "He's bound and determined to talk me out of my drawers. I can't stall him much longer."

A moment passed, then Tallman shrugged. "String him along somehow. All I can do is dig deeper, and that'll take time."

"Where will you dig that you haven't already dug?"

"Frankly"—Tallman rocked his head from side to side—"I wish to hell I knew."

"Oh, great." Vivian regarded him with brash impudence. "You're some comfort in my hour of trial."

"Don't make it sound like a melodrama."

"Why not? I'm facing a fate worse than death—*tonight.*"

"Tonight?"

"I'm having dinner with Harland and his hard-on. He

insisted and I couldn't weasel out of it. You might say we're too well-acquainted—after two days."

"So we're back to square one."

"Pardon me?"

"The basics," Tallman observed wryly. "Tonight, I start tailing Ordway."

A short while after ten that evening, a hansom cab halted in front of the hotel. Harlan Ordway hopped out with the randy enthusiasm of a young goat. Then he assisted Vivian down as though she were some priceless objet d'art. His grin was jack-o-lantern wide.

Vivian took his arm and they strolled into the hotel. A bellman scampered toward the elevator as they crossed the lobby. Ordway looked proud as punch, and his chest was swelled out like a pouter pigeon. He doffed his hat and bowed her into the elevator. The door closed and the bellman rotated the control lever. The elevator lumbered upward.

Ordway had every reason to expect a favorable conclusion to the evening. Vivian wore a velvet grown, her shoulders bare and the décolletage dipping low to reveal the vee of her breasts. He'd wined her and dined her at the town's swankiest restaurant, and not once had their conversation touched on business matters. All evening she had flirted with him outrageously, her voice intimate and her eyes provocative. He had no doubt that tonight was his night.

On the third floor, Ordway escorted her to the door of her suite. She removed the key from her beaded evening bag and his pulsebeat quickened. She unlocked the door and turned to face him so abruptly he was taken off guard. She went up on tiptoe and kissed him lightly on the cheek.

"I had a marvelous time, Harland. Simply marvelous!"

Ordway gave her a bewildered look. "Aren't you going to invite me in for a nightcap?"

"Naughty boy," Vivian said with a teasing lilt. "You have more on your mind than a nightcap."

"I thought—" Ordway faltered, then went on lamely. "Well, after tonight, I thought we were . . . that is to say . . . the attraction was mutual."

"You are a goose!" Vivian cocked her head with a seductive little smile. "I'm attracted to you more than I dare let myself admit."

"I don't understand." Ordway looked abjectly uncomfortable. "We're both adults and—"

"Hush, now!" Vivian eyes shone with a clear virginal light. "All in good time, Harlan. Don't rush me and spoil it . . . pretty please?"

Ordway appeared on the verge of saying something, but evidently changed is mind. Vivian waited, watching him with a look of coquettish amusement. Then she kissed her fingers and touched them to his lips.

"Adieu for now . . . darling man."

The door closed and Ordway stood alone in the hallway. He threw up his hands in exasperation and limped toward the elevator. His balls ached like frozen stones.

Outside the hotel, Ordway appeared indecisive. There were no cabs about and the street was empty. He finally crossed the square and stumped off toward the south side of town. His expression was vaguely disoriented.

Tallman stepped from the doorway of a darkened store. He was somewhat puzzled by the direction Ordway had taken. The south side of town was considered the wrong side of the tracks, the sporting district. The thought occurred that Ordway was frustrated, hurting for a woman, and meant to let off steam at a local cathouse. Yet his impression of Ordway was not that of a man who consorted with whores. He followed along half a block behind.

Ordway went directly to a saloon on the south side. Low-class and seedy, the joint was frequented by the town's rougher element. On the street, Tallman paused and watched through a dirt-specked window. He saw a slender, shifty-eyed man move from behind the bar and greet Ordway. They exchanged a few words, and then the man signaled a second bartender and tossed his apron on the counter. His causal air of authority left little doubt that he owned the dive. He nodded to Ordway and led the way to a back room. The door opened and closed in a glare of lamplight.

Tallman was to think some time afterward that life took funny turns. A curious blend of luck and coincidence, rather than hard-nosed detective work, had led him here tonight. He crossed the street and moved into a shadowed doorway.

Late that night, Tallman and Vivian sat talking in her suite. He'd tailed Ordway home, after leaving the saloon, and then returned to the hotel. He was somewhat mystified by the turn of events, not at all sure what it meant. But his mood was almost euphoric.

"One thing's for certain," he said with a slow grin. "Ordway wasn't there to drown his sorrows. He was there on business."

"What sort of business?"

"Lowdown and dirty," Tallman told her. "That saloon-keeper looked like he'd cut your throat and never turn a hair. Very strange company for a man with Ordway's spotless reputation."

"God, I hope you're right," Vivian sighed. "We're certainly due for a break."

"Long overdue," Tallman added. "But I think we're finally on to something. Ordway wouldn't meet with a character like that unless it was important. So important they had their heads together for over an hour."

"Okay, chief," Vivian responded brightly. "Where do we go from here?"

Tallman rocked back on the sofa with a great belly laugh. "Starting tomorrow, I'll stick to that saloonkeeper like glue. Your job's to diddle Ordway along and keep him occupied."

Vivian groaned. "His pants are on fire now. How do you suggest I cool him down?"

"You'll outfox him somehow."

"Not forever," Vivian said fiercely. "You'd better wrap things up fast—damned fast!"

Tallman's features took on a distant, prophetic look. He stared off into space, silent a moment. Then a ghost of a smile tugged at the corner of his mouth.

"Don't worry, Viv. I intend to do just that."

FIFTEEN

A late afternoon sun filtered through the grimy window. The saloon appeared to be a hangout for grifters and hustlers, and those on the lower rung of the sporting crowd. The men lining the bar took their whiskey neat and amused themselves swapping dirty stories. None of them looked like they were hunting honest work.

Tallman sat alone at a table toward the rear. His disguise was that of a grungy drifter with a taste for the sauce. He wore an oversized jacket and baggy trousers, topped off by a battered slouch hat. His face was covered by a matted beard, which was plastered on with spirit gum and gave him the look of a tumbleweed with eyes. Before him on the crude table were a shot glass and a bottle of rotgut. A roll-your-own dangled from his lip, trailing wisps of smoke.

Earlier, not long after noon, Tallman had wandered into the saloon. His unsavory appearance fitted perfectly with the dive's clientele, and he was soon lost in the crowd. He staked out one of the back tables and ordered a bottle, paying from a crumpled wad of greenbacks. He spoke to no one, playing the part of a surly loner, and no one spoke to him. He evidenced no interest in the conversation or dirty stories, and seldom looked up from the table. His attention seemed fixed on the bottle, and some inward dialogue known only to himself. Yet his eyes were alert, and watchful.

By eavesdropping, he'd learned that the saloon-keeper's name was Jack Porter. Upon closer examination, he had also discovered that Porter seemed born to the role of a cutthroat. The shifty eyes were sunk deep within a gargoyle face, complete with hooked nose and a down-turned mouth. The saloon crowd treated him with wary respect, though he was slender and hardly more than average height. Considering the rough nature of the crowd, it was a telling comment. Jack Porter was apparently an ugly customer when crossed, perhaps a stone-cold killer. Quite clearly, no one crossed him in his own joint.

Toward sundown, Tallman got the break he'd waited for all afternoon. The door swung open and a thick-shouldered bruiser entered the saloon. He was swarthy, with splayed cheekbones and sleek, glistening hair. He wore rough work clothes and mule-eared boots; the bulge of a pistol was obvious beneath his coat. He walked to the rear of the bar and stopped, waiting with a sort of brutish patience. Porter gave the other bartender the high sign and they huddled in a brief conversation. Then the saloonkeeper untied his apron and moved along the counter. He stepped past the end of the bar and nodded to the bruiser.

"Cobb."

"Hullo, Jack."

"You set to go?"

"I reckon I am."

Tallman was within earshot, and instantly on edge. Out of the corner of his eye, he watched Porter and Cobb disappear into the back room. A sudden impulse told him it was time to move. He downed his drink, then hitched back his chair and walked from the saloon. Outside, he crossed the street to a deserted alleyway. There he stripped off the beard and tossed it into a trash barrel. He was still rubbing spirit gum off his face when Porter and Cobb emerged from an alley beside the saloon. Both men carried heavy suitcases, and they turned west onto a sidestreet. He tailed them from some distance behind.

A short walk brought them to the train depot. Tallman waited outside while the men purchased tickets. When they went through the door to the platform, he entered and paid the fare to San Francisco. Whatever their destination, the ticket covered him to the end of the line. He hung around inside, leery of being spotted even though he'd removed the beard. Presently, the evening north bound arrived and the two men, along with several other passengers, boarded the coaches. He delayed until the very last moment and then hurried across the platform.

He jumped aboard as the train pulled out of Bakersfield.

Sometime after midnight the train slowed outside Fresno. Porter and Cobb collected their bags from the overhead rack and walked to the rear of the car. A few moments later the coaches screeched to a halt in front of the station house.

Tallman was slumped down in a seat beside the window. He waited, watching from beneath the brim of his slouch hat, until they rounded the corner of the depot. Then, as though galvanized, he bounded from his seat and ran for the door. Outside, he moved swiftly to the end of the platform and peeked around the corner. Porter and Cobb were ambling along the sidewalk with no apparent haste. Their general direction was toward the uptown business district.

So far, Tallman was at a loss to explain their movements. He hadn't the vaguest notion of where they were headed and even less idea as to why they had detrained in Fresno. To all appearances, they were a couple of weary travelers off in search of a hotel room for the night. Yet some visceral instinct told him their trip was no spur of the moment thing. All he'd seen, and the little he had overheard in the saloon, convinced him the two men were here for a purpose. He thought they'd been ordered here by Harlan Ordway.

A block from the business district, Porter and Cobb turned on to a sidestreet. When Tallman reached the corner and took a quick look, the men had vanished. He increased his stride, checking the doorways of warehouses and commercial buildings as he went along. Halfway down the block, he paused at the mouth of an alley and cautiously inched his head around the corner of a building. He saw Porter and Cobb emerge on the next street over, briefly silhouetted against the light from a lamppost. Then they wheeled left and disappeared from view.

Tallman was bewildered by their erratic behavior. But he quickly developed a grudging admiration for their technique. Over the next ten minutes, the men played a very skillful game of cat and mouse. The path they followed was filled with twists and turns, dodging into alleys and rushing along sidestreets, as though wending their way through a maze. Yet, despite their random movements, it slowly became apparent they were doubling back. For every false turn, there was another shift that led southwest, toward the outskirts of town. The chase ended at the Southern Pacific railway yards.

A pale sickle moon dimly lighted the sky. Visible in the spectral glow was a labyrinth of tracks and switching-gates. Spread out over several acres, the yards were a holding area for railway rolling stock. Line upon line of boxcars, flatbeds and passenger coaches stood like ghostly columns in the still night. There was little activity, for the hour was late and the locomotives used to stage trains generally went into operation shortly before dawn. Across the way, there was a flicker of lantern light as the watchman made his rounds. Otherwise the yards lay cloaked in eerie darkness.

Hidden in the shadows of a warehouse, Tallman waited at the edge of the yards. A sudden foreboding crept over him as he watched Porter and Cobb cross a stretch of open tracks. He was no longer in doubt as to the purpose of their trip, and the contents of their suitcases abruptly ceased to be a mystery. The moon went behind a cloud and he lost sight of them for a moment. Then the light reappeared and he spotted their dim figures, apparitions in the gloom. Quietly, moving with great stealth, they slipped behind a row of flatbed cars.

Somewhat unsettled, Tallman swiftly considered the

options. His first instinct was to go after them and stop them, somehow abort their mission. Yet he suppressed the urge and forced himself to think it through. Stalking men at night was tricky business. Sounds were magnified, and even pale moonlight increased the odds of being spotted. He might spook the men and end up in a footchase. Once they dropped the suitcases and ran, it would be his word against theirs, with no solid proof of criminal intent. Nor would there be any practical means of linking them to Harlan Ordway. All of which brought him to the only remaining option. However destructive, Porter and Cobb must be allowed to complete their night's work. The idea was repugnant, but he willed himself to let it happen. He edged deeper into the shadows, and waited.

Several minutes later a southbound freight train loomed out of the dark. The engine's headlamp played over the tracks as the train rolled slowly through the yards. In the distance, Tallman saw a flare of matches behind the row of parked flatbeds. Then, almost simultaneously, two explosive fuses sputtered to life between the flatbeds and a nearby row of passenger coaches. Porter and Cobb suddenly materialized out of the dark and took off running across the tracks. Their timing was flawless, coordinated perfectly with the freight train moving through Fresno. Side by side, they approached the train and swung themselves through the open door of a boxcar. The caboose trundled past the yards a moment later.

Tallman stepped out of the shadows and sprinted hard. He pulled abreast of the caboose, gauging his stride, and hopped aboard. From the steps, he moved onto the rear platform and mounted the steel ladder which led to the roof. Once on top, he took a moment to get a feel for the rocking motion of the train. Then, with some sense of balance, he walked forward as the caboose cleared the outskirts of town. He leaped from car to car, hurrying now as the train began to pick up speed. On his fourth leap, he landed on the roof of the empty boxcar. He went belly down and crawled toward the open door.

The sky was suddenly lighted by an earsplitting blast. The force of the explosion instantly transformed the railway yards into a tangled mass of steel and wood. A towering ball of fire leaped skyward and the concussion shook the earth. All the rolling stock within a hundred yards of the blast simply disintegrated, littering the ground with charred and mangled wreckage. Flames licked through the ruins, jumping from car to car, and within seconds the railway yards were enveloped in a raging holocaust. As though some diabolic force had scorched the land, there was nothing left but a smoldering pyre of debris. A billowing cloud of smoke rose from the devastation, blotting out the moon.

Tallman lay flattened out on the roof of the boxcar. He stared at the distant flames, stunned by the cyclonic force of the explosion. A fleeting thought passed through his mind, and he concluded that some combination of nitro and dynamite had been used in the bombing. Then he heard laughter and shouts from inside the boxcar, and realized the bombers were congratulating one another on a job well done. Their whopping jerked him out of his daze and reminded him that his night's work was far from complete. He wormed to the other side of the boxcar and found a handhold on the roof. Feet first, he lowered himself over the edge and swung through the open door. He landed on his knees and rolled, drawing the Colt.

"Don't move!" he ordered, rising to one knee. "I want you alive!"

Porter and Cobb were framed in the opposite doorway, their backs to him. A split second elapsed, then both men pulled their guns and spun around. Porter was a hair faster, and Tallman shot him above the belt buckle. He stumbled sideways, clutching at his gut, then keeled over and fell sprawled out on the floor. Cobb got off a hurried snap-shot, which thunked into the far wall. Arm extended, Tallman triggered three blasts in rapid succession. The impact of the slugs drove Cobb backwards through the open door. His hands clawed at empty air and he hung suspended a moment in space. The train rushed past and he slipped from view.

Tallman stood and walked forward. He stopped and kicked Porter's gun aside. Then he went down on one knee, the Colt dangling loosely from his hand. Porter's arms were wrapped around his stomach and his eyes were glazed with pain. He searched Tallman's face with a glassy stare.

"You a railroad dick?"

"Does it matter?"

"No . . . guess not."

"Listen close, Porter." Tallman's voice was edged. "How would you like to live?"

Porter blinked, swallowed hard. "Where'd you get my name?"

"You're not listening," Tallman said flatly. "You've got

a choice between the boneyard and living to a ripe old age. Which will it be?"

"I—" Porter's face twisted in a grimace. "I dunno what you're talkin' about."

"It's simple enough," Tallman said with ominous calm. "I want some information. You answer my questions and I'll stop the train at the next town. A doctor will have you patched up in no time."

"You on the square?"

"I suppose you'll have to take my word, won't you?"

"Awright." Porter spoke through clenched teeth.

"Who hired you to blow the railyard?"

"Harlan Ordway."

"What about the other bombings?" Tallman demanded. "Was he behind those too?"

"Yeah," Porter said, his voice clogged. "Tonight was our fourth job."

"Why the Southern Pacific?" Tallman's expression was wooden. "What was his purpose?"

"I dunno," Porter grunted, shook his head. "Never asked and he never told me. Strictly a cash-and-carry deal."

Tallman's eyes hooded. "What about the Settlers' League? Major McQuade?"

"I never heard of neither one."

"How about the strip of land southeast of Bakersfield? What's that got to do with Ordway and the bombings?"

Porter gave him a walleyed look. "What land?"

"Don't dummy up on me."

"I ain't!" Porter's face suddenly went chalky. "Jesus, how far's the next town? I'm hurtin' bad, awful bad."

"You haven't told me about that strip of land."

"I done told you all I know."

"You're lying!"

"Why would I—"

All the blood leeched out of Porter's features. An icy shudder swept over him and the light went out in his eyes. His mouth opened in a long sigh and his sphincter voided with a stench. One boot heel drummed the floor in after-death. Then he lay still.

Tallman cursed and quickly checked for a pulse. After a moment he stood, holstering the Colt, and walked to the door. He stared out into the night, assailed by a sense of time running ahead of him. Without a witness, he was stalemated, back where he'd started. Worse, he'd established no link between Ordway and McQuade, the Settlers' League and the railroad. And he had only himself to blame.

SIXTEEN

Vivian was beside herself with worry. For the past two nights, Ordway had courted her like a schoolboy afflicted with puppy love. He'd squired her around town, treating her to lavish dinners complete with champagne and candlelight. Her hotel suite was so filled with flowers it resembled a botanical garden. And not once had he attempted to force himself on her.

She thought it was too good to last. Time was the enemy, and her coy response to his advances was fast losing its charm. Tonight she was dressed in another off-the-shoulder gown, and the candlelight cast a creamy, alabaster glow over her full breasts. Yet, for all her seductive efforts, Ordway was in a bearish mood. He sat across the table, swilling champagne, and his eyes were etched with a look of mounting frustration. She knew he wouldn't wait much longer.

Harlan Ordway, however, was only part of her dilemma. Her greater concern centered on Tallman's strange disappearance. Yesterday, operating in disguise, he'd undertaken surveillance of the southside saloonkeeper. Last night, when he hadn't returned to the hotel, she was only moderately worried. A surveillance often turned into an around-the-clock job, and she naturally assumed he'd stuck with the suspect. But today the newspaper had bannered the story of last night's bombing in Fresno. Since it involved the railway yards, she quite reasonably believed there was a connection with Tallman's unexplained absence. All the more worrisome, the newspaper revealed that the bodies of two men had been found along the tracks, some miles south of the railway yards. So far neither of the dead men had been identified.

Vivian was forced to consider a grim prospect. It was entirely possible that Tallman had tailed the saloonkeeper to Fresno, and witnessed the bombing. Then, carrying the premise a step further, it was equally plausible that Tallman had suffered a mortal wound in the act of killing the saloonkeeper. She was filled with dread and uncertainty, and some part of her refused to believe he was dead. Yet, however grisly, the likelihood was too real to ignore. It would account for two unidentified bodies—and Tallman's disappearance.

Unnerved by the prospect, Vivian clung to a faint hope. She loved him deeply, and though to her religion was a sometimes thing, she prayed for his safe return. Still, in the event he was dead, that merely underscored the need to get on with the investigation, and bring down the man responsible. Harlan Ordway spent three days showing her land and three nights trying to cajole her into bed, but she hadn't uncovered an iota of evidence. She sensed that it was tonight or never. He was grumpy and disillusioned, and only a bold play on her part would reverse the situation. She decided to risk everything on a daring gambit.

"Harlan?"

"Yes."

"I'm worried about my investment program."

"Do we have to talk business?" Ordway said with a flare of annoyance. "I get quite enough of that during the day."

"That's just the point!" Vivian exclaimed. "We've wasted the last three days—and all for nothing."

"Wasted!" Ordway looked up sharply. "At some personal expense, I've ignored my own business affairs and devoted myself to your interests. I hardly consider it time wasted."

"Oh, pshaw!" Vivian's tone was light and mocking. "You needn't be so touchy. I only meant to say we haven't found any suitable land."

"No fault of mine," Ordway grouched. "I've shown you most of Kern County and quoted you prices lower than the going rate. You're a very hard woman to please."

"Yes, that's true." Vivian smiled, as if sharing a private joke with herself. "I'm particular in all things, investments as well as men."

Ordway grunted, and tossed off a glass of champagne. "I'd be the first to vouch for that."

"Don't be nasty," Vivian chided him. "The fact remains, you've shown me most of Kern County, but not all."

"You've seen all that amounts to anything."

"I wonder." Vivian stared at him questioningly. "Before you arrived this morning, I was waiting in the lobby and a gentleman engaged me in conversation. One thing led to another and we began talking land. He suggested I look southeast of town."

"Southeast?" Surprise washed over Ordway's face. "Who was he?"

"I'm terrible on names," Vivian said ingenuously. "But he seemed to know what he was talking about. He said the land there is undervalued and represents an excellent long term investment."

"Nonsense," Ordway said gruffly. "Why do you think I haven't shown you anything to the southeast? It's practically a desert, absolutely worthless."

Vivian lifted an eyebrow. "Harlan, answer me truthfully. Do you own land there?"

"Well . . ." Ordway paused, cleared his throat. "I own a few parcels, strictly a speculative venture."

"There, you see!" Vivian looked hurt. "It's a good investment after all! You haven't been candid with me, Harlan."

"No, I assure you," Ordway said evasively, "it's not what you think."

"Now you've gone and spoiled everything."

"What do you mean? Spoiled what?"

Vivian put on her best pout. "I had plans for tonight."

"Plans for"—Ordway's lips peeled back in a weak smile—"for later?"

"Yes." Vivian lowered her voice, eyes downcast. "But I could never . . . be friendly . . . with a man who doesn't trust me. I simply couldn't."

"I *do* trust you." Ordway flushed with ardor. "I swear it."

"Then you'll tell me about the land—no secrets?"

"I might," Ordway said gingerly. "Later tonight, perhaps."

Vivian knew what would happen at the hotel. The thought was repulsive, but she had exhausted her options. It was time to negotiate with sex.

Only one lamp was lighted in the suite. The wick was turned down and the sitting room was bathed in an umber glow. Ordway had her pinned in the corner of the sofa, and his hands were busy. He'd consumed enough champagne to embalm a corpse, but with no apparent effect on his passion. His kisses were wet and a hard knot bulged his trousers.

"Oh, really!" Vivian squirmed part way loose. "You're so impatient, Harlan!"

"Your fault," Ordway muttered. "You made me wait forever."

"Now, behave yourself!" Vivian tweaked his nose. "We haven't had our talk yet."

"Talk?"

"Yes, about the land."

"Later!" Ordway feverishly kissed her neck. "I need you now!"

"You promise?"

"On a stack of bibles!"

"Well . . ."

Vivian dropped the front of her gown with a quick tug. Her breasts stood out proudly, coral-tipped and beautifully shaped. Ordway stared at them a moment, pop-eyed with wonder. Then his mouth opened and he buried his head in the warm mounds. His lips closed over a nipple and he sucked like a greedy bee drawing nectar. His tongue was slick and moist and never still.

"Ooooh Harlan!" Vivian murmured. "You're wonderful!"

Her hand went to his trousers. She unbuttoned his fly and pulled down his shorts. His cock jumped out like a one-eyed monster, rigid and stiff. She grasped it and squeezed and began to stroke gently. He groaned and suddenly flopped back on the sofa, paralyzed with lust.

"Harlan?"

"Ummm . . ."

Her hand bobbed up and down. "Why is that land a good investment?"

"Ahhh, Jesus!"

Her stroke quickened. "Tell me and I'll kiss it—the French way."

Ordway moaned. "A railroad charter."

"And you own the right-of-way?"

"Ummm . . ."

Her hand rode his rod. "How soon will it be built?"

"Sweet Jesus!" Ordway hunched upward. "A year . . . less."

"And it's certain to go through, absolutely certain?"

"Yessss!"

Her hand pumped three rapid-fire strokes. His cock quivered and suddenly spurted a thick milky jet of come up the front of his vest. There was a moment of stark silence. Then he exhaled a long sigh and opened his eyes. He looked down at his vest with an expression of doglike disbelief.

"Ooh!" Vivian cooed. "What a shame!"

His manhood shriveled, went limp in her hand. She neatly tucked him away and slipped the bodice of her gown up over her breasts. Then she graced him with a dazzling smile.

"Don't fret, Harlan. You'll do better tomorrow night."

A short time after Ordway left there was a knock at the door. Vivian thought she was rid of him for the night and she uttered a soft curse. Searching her mind for a new excuse, she put on a smile and opened the door. Tallman stepped into the suite.

Vivian's heart almost stopped. She squealed with relief and threw herself into his arms. She was crying and laughing and peppering him with kisses all at the same time. He embraced her warmly and assured her he was still very much alive. She hung on, her arms locked around his neck, as though she might awake and discover it was all a dream. Finally, with some effort, he calmed her fears and got her seated on the sofa. She composed herself and listened while he talked.

Tallman quickly recounted the events of the previous night. Following the shootout, and Porter's confession, he'd tossed the body out of the boxcar. At Delano, a town further down the line, he had hopped off the freight train and checked into a hotel. Early that evening, rested by several hours sleep, he had boarded a passenger train and proceeded to Bakersfield. Under cover of darkness, he had made his way to the hotel and changed clothes in his room. Then he'd taken a seat in the lobby, waiting to make certain she was alone. The moment Ordway departed, he had come straightaway to the suite.

"That's it," he concluded. "With Porter dead, we've got no proof that Ordway ordered the bombings. And nothing whatever that ties him to McQuade and the Settlers' League. No witness, no proof and no case."

"But we've got a motive." Vivian's eyes glittered like candles in a pumpkin. "I persuaded Ordway to talk about the land southeast of town."

"Well?"

"Hold on to your hat." Vivian giggled. "Someone has a charter to build a railroad to Bakersfield. Ordway bought that land to provide a clear right-of-way."

Tallman stared at her in mild astonishment. "A railroad from where?"

"I've no idea," Vivian shrugged. "He wasn't too free with details and I was afraid to push it. I quit while I was ahead."

"Hmmm." Tallman watched her with an odd smile. "How'd you get him to talk?"

Vivian's laugh was low and infectious. "Let's just say I conned him with a little femme and a little fatale."

"How much femme?"

"Oh, enough." Vivian's eyes shuttled away. "I got my hands dirty, but my honor's still intact."

"Say no more." Tallman grinned and squeezed her leg. "Ordway will never know what he missed."

"Horny bastard!" Vivian said vehemently. "I had to promise him a return engagement tomorrow night. Otherwise he'd still be here!"

"You're off the hook," Tallman said, suddenly sober. "I

wired Otis Blackburn from Delano. In so many words, I let him know it had to do with last night's bombing. He wired back and ordered us to San Francisco. We're scheduled to meet with him tomorrow afternoon."

"What do you think he has in mind?"

"I imagine he plans to roast our coals. As you'll recall, our assignment was to stop the Settlers' League . . . and the bombings."

"But the settlers aren't responsible."

"Exactly," Tallman nodded seriously. "So we have to convince him there's more to this conspiracy than anyone suspected."

"Easy to say," Vivian noted with an intense look. "But we're still very much in the dark ourselves."

Tallman considered a moment. "Let's try a bit of supposition and see where it leads. As an example, suppose someone wanted to break the Southern Pacific's stranglehold on central and southern California. Wouldn't the first step be to establish a competing railway line?"

"It's been tried before," Vivian observed. "The Southern Pacific undercuts their rates and forces them into a price war and *poof!* There goes the competition."

"Let me rephrase the question." Tallman's features creased in a frown. "Suppose someone wanted to *destroy* the Southern Pacific in lower California? Not a rival railroad, no competition—but destroy them."

Vivian caught her breath. "It wouldn't work without public support. So our theoretical 'someone' starts a farmers' revolt and then nudges it along until it turns into a statewide rebellion. Am I close?"

"Very close." The lines on Tallman's forehead deepened.

"Someone bides his time awaiting an opportune moment. The Southern Pacific finally creates the perfect issue by attempting to evict the farmers in Hanford. At that point, Major McQuade appears Johnny-on-the-spot. He organizes the Settlers' League and leads them into battle—a holy crusade against the Octopus."

"Complete with sabotage," Vivian added. "The Southern Pacific blames the League for the bombings. And McQuade tells the settlers it's a plot—the railroad sabotaging itself—simply to discredit the League. All carefully orchestrated to win public support and divert attention away from the ultimate objective: a new railroad."

"A really diabolical scheme," Tallman said with a trace of admiration. "Well conceived and brilliantly executed, the work of a mastermind."

"Are you talking about Ordway?"

Tallman was quiet, a long pause of inner deliberation. "Ordway will make a fortune on the sale of the right-of-way. Whether or not he's the mastermind remains to be seen. A scheme this elaborate required someone with an extensive knowledge of railroads."

"I almost forgot!" Vivian sat upright. "Ordway told me the railroad will be built in a year or less. Does that mean anything?"

"I'd say it's perfect timing. A year will allow the rebellion to spread and create a public outcry for a new railroad. Our 'someone' probably already has the roadbed surveyed."

"Sounds like they're operating on a schedule."

"Yes, it all fits." Tallman hesitated, slowly shaking his head. "One thing still has me puzzled though. Why a charter to the southeast? It would be a railroad to nowhere."

"Perhaps they don't care," Vivian said with a sweeping gesture. "Maybe it's just a way to get a foot in the door and spread out from there. A bunco artist would call it the flash—the come-on!"

"Highbinders employ somewhat the same tactic."

"Highbinders?"

Tallman's mouth curled in a sardonic smile. "That's what these westerners call someone who's underhanded and vicious by nature."

Vivian's voice rippled with laughter. "I think you just described our employers."

"We'll find out tomorrow—in San Francisco."

SEVENTEEN

McQuade is nothing more than a front man."

"So it would seem."

"Harlan Ordway's the one we have to nail."

"You're convinced he's the ringleader?"

"I am."

"Why?"

"Because everything dovetails."

Tallman and Vivian were seated in Otis Blackburn's office. Late that afternoon they had arrived in San Francisco and gone directly to the Southern Pacific headquarters on Montgomery Street. From the outset, it had been apparent that the general superintendent was boiling mad. He held them responsible for the Fresno bombing.

Thus far, Tallman had acted as spokesman. He'd delivered a report on their investigation, fitting the pieces together into a broad mosaic. Vivian had stayed in the background, saying nothing, all too aware of Blackburn's contempt for lady detectives. She watched now as the two men stared at each other across the desk.

"I agree," Blackburn said at length. "Ordway's admission to Miss Valentine corroborates everything you learned the night of the bombing. I regret you found it necessary to kill Porter. His testimony would have made our case."

"At the time," Tallman said with exaggerated gravity, "I saw no alternative. He was trying to kill me."

Blackburn nodded, pursing his lips. "What about McQuade? Suppose we were to offer him immunity from prosecution. Would he turn state's evidence?"

"Not in my opinion," Tallman allowed. "He doesn't strike me as a turncoat. Quite the opposite, in fact."

"How do you suggest we proceed, then?"

"By the back door," Tallman explained. "We know Ordway's involved in a railroad scheme. Somehow, we have to link that to the sabotage and the overall conspiracy. I'm convinced Ordway isn't acting alone. The scope of it is too big—too ambitious."

"Bigger than you think," Blackburn pointed out. "We've known for some time that the Santa Fe plans to extend track from New Mexico to California. It's all hush-hush, very secretive, but we have our sources. Their goal is to establish a second transcontinental line. We had no idea the project was so far along . . . until today."

"Now it makes sense!" Tallman's eyes widened. "That strip of land to the southeast provides the Santa Fe with a right-of-way into California. Ordway makes a fortune and Bakersfield becomes the terminus on a new transcontinental route. All of southern California would then have a direct outlet to the eastern markets. No wonder they organized a farmers' revolt."

"Exactly," Blackburn said in a crisp tone. "But that

makes the threat far more serious than we thought. The Santa Fe has to be stopped before its tracks reach the California border. As of this moment, I'm broadening your original assignment."

"To include the Santa Fe?"

"Only indirectly," Blackburn informed him. "I want proof that Harlan Ordway engineered a criminal conspiracy. Once we have him under indictment, our problems are solved. We'll tar the Santa Fe with the same brush and stop them cold."

"Ordway's a slippery character," Tallman remarked. "Without witnesses, we need something tangible in the way of evidence. We might have to take a new tack—extralegal means."

"Your methods don't interest me. I want an indictment and I want it damned fast! Then we'll turn our attention to the Settlers' League."

Tallman looked surprised, then suddenly irritated. "Perhaps I failed to make myself clear. Ordway and McQuade are the ones we're after. The settlers were strictly dupes, innocent bystanders. They had no part in the conspiracy or the sabotage."

Blackburn waved the thought aside. "Dupes or not, they're dangerous to the Southern Pacific. We intend to make an object lesson of them, and in no uncertain terms. We want the farmers' rebellion to end there!"

"How do you plan to accomplish that?"

"You are to wire me," Blackburn ordered, "once you have the goods on Ordway. I'll then arrange for Sheriff Wilcox and a couple of our men to meet you. Wilcox will explain the plan at that time."

"I think not," Tallman said in a measured tone. "I told you before I won't work with hired guns. Nothing's happened to change my mind."

Blackburn unfolded a letter and tossed it across the desk. "Here's the latest word from Allan Pinkerton. Considering your attitude at our last meeting, I figured we ought to establish who's in charge. The letter speaks for itself."

Tallman quickly scanned the contents. The message was unequivocal and bluntly stated. He was directed to follow Blackburn's instructions and complete the assignment to the client's satisfaction. No excuses would be tolerated. His mouth tightened and he took an instant to collect himself. Then he gave Blackburn a long, slow look.

"You've snookered me pretty good."

"So good," Blackburn said with vinegary satisfaction, "that you'd be wise to play along. I gather Pinkerton doesn't approve of agents who exercise their own judgment."

"We'll take it a step at a time."

"What does that mean?"

"It means we'll get the evidence on Ordway—and go from there."

"Obey my instructions," Blackburn said, his head angled critically, "or you may find yourself out of a job."

"You've got your money's worth so far."

"So far doesn't count," Blackburn said curtly. "We're talking about what's to come."

"Hide and watch," Tallman said with a clenched smile. "You'll be the first to know."

"I warn you—"

Tallman stood and walked from the room. On his heels, Vivian turned at the door and flipped Blackburn a saucy salute. The door closed with a soft click.

Outside the building, Tallman and Vivian paused on Montgomery Street. Dusk was settling over the city and the business district was all but deserted. Tallman lit a cigar and puffed angry clouds of smoke. His eyes were like chips of quartz.

"Damn Pinkerton anyway!"

"What did you expect?" Vivian asked reasonably. "He's built his reputation on loyalty to the client."

"Blind loyalty!" Tallman fumed. "Doesn't he know Blackburn's the original son of a bitch? Christ, anybody would!"

Vivian was silent a moment. "Do you intend to follow orders?"

"Oh, we'll get Ordway and McQuade. But the settlers are another matter entirely. They deserve a fair shake."

"Ash, be realistic." Vivian's voice was soft and troubled. "Either you deliver or Pinkerton has no choice but to assign another operative. So it's really an exercise in pragmatics. If you don't do it, somebody else will."

"I suppose," Tallman agreed reluctantly. "Of course, that's not to say I have to deliver them body and soul. Something less than a crucifixion might do."

Vivian looked at him with utter directness. "Blackburn's no fool, so don't get too cute. You're no help to the settlers unless you remain on the case."

Tallman was quiet so long she began to think he

wouldn't answer. But he finally took a long pull on his cigar and his mood seemed to change. A lazy smile spread over his face.

"I need a diversion."

"Anything particular in mind?"

"How about dinner in Chinatown?"

"Sounds good."

"And I know just the place." Tallman laughed. Vivian tucked her hand in his arm and they walked off into the dusk.

The Street of a Thousand Lanterns teemed with people. Otherwise known as Washington Street, the central thoroughfare of Chinatown reeked with the sweet smell of opium and the oppressive aroma of sweaty bodies. Women wore floppy pantaloons and long smocks, and the men were dressed in long jackets and baggy pajama pants, their hair braided in pigtails. Sidewalk shops displaying pickled squid and skinned ducks merely added to the rank odor.

Crib whores, the lowest form of slave girls, bartered their wares openly. Behind barred windows, they stood in their squalid cubicles, offering themselves to passersby in a singsong chant. Naked from the waist down, they wore only short blouses, and their trade was conducted at bargain rates. A customer who cared to check out the plumbing paid six bits upon entering the crib. His stay was short, for the girls were fast workers and operated on the principle of quick turnover. Their clientele consisted mostly of drunken sailors, freshly arrived in port. Business was brisk tonight.

Vivian was all eyes. Tallman smiled, amused by her fascination with the crib girls and their approach to the oldest profession. While they walked, he explained that Chinatown was actually a city within a city. The district was the largest Chinese settlement outside the Orient, and the culture of Old Cathay still prevailed. Some thirty thousand people lived and worked within a dozen square blocks, and seldom set foot in the white man's San Francisco. Frugal and industrious, they followed their own customs and made only surface concessions to the outside world. To enter Chinatown was to step backward in time.

Their destination was the Jade Palace. The owner, who wore a silk mandarin gown and a black skullcap, greeted them profusely. His deferential manner indicated that Tallman was no stranger to the place. They were escorted along a corridor and ushered into a room with sliding doors. One part of the room was a bedchamber and the other part was a dining area, with a low teakwood table surrounded by plush cushions. The walls were decorated with silk prints and the floor was covered by a rich Oriental carpet. The scent of joss sticks filled the air with a heady, intoxicating aroma.

"Ash Tallman!" Vivian laughed and glanced at the bed. "Fun and games the Chinese way. Aren't you the sly one?"

"Viv, the best is yet to come!"

Somewhere a zither struck up a haunting melody. Then serving girls glided spectrally into the room, laden with dishes and trays. The meal was one exotic delight after another. The girls served prawns and pork, cooked in delicate sauces, complimented by steamy bowls of vegetables faintly reminiscent of spiced seaweed. With each course, there was another vial of rice wine, mild to the palate and deceptively potent. The meal was lavish and unhurried, every bite a savory experience. And always there was another vial of rice wine.

While they ate, Tallman explained that Orientals were very sensual people. Food was merely one aspect of sensual pleasure, a prelude of sorts. In fact, the Chinese were connoisseurs of the flesh, and generally considered whites to be a sexually backward race. A Chinese man, whether married or not, wouldn't dream of limiting himself to one woman. For their part, Chinese women took great pride in inventive foreplay and ancient techniques passed along from generation to generation. Nowhere outside the Orient was there such a preoccupation with sex, and a reverent appreciation of eroticism. The Chinese treated lovemaking as one of the higher art forms.

After dinner, the table was cleared and the serving girls disappeared. Vivian was light-headed with wine and tingling with anticipation. The atmosphere, combined with Tallman's discourse on things sensual, had put her in a sexy mood. She leaned across the table and took his hand. Her eyes gleamed with invitation.

The door suddenly opened and a Chinese girl of evocative beauty stepped into the room. She was tiny, with a breathlessly slim waist and firm, youthful breasts. Her complexion was honey gold, and her almond-shaped eyes were framed by hair the color of obsidian. She wore a cream white kimono that hugged her body like melted ivory. She closed the door and bowed, her mouth curved in an enigmatic smile. Then she extended her hand to Vivian.

"Ash—?"

"Let her help you." Tallman waved his wine cup. "It's the custom."

Vivian rose a bit uncertainly from her floor cushion. She accepted the girl's hand and allowed herself to be led to the bedchamber. There the girl assisted her out of her gown and undergarments, all the while admiring her voluptuous figure. When she was naked, the girl helped her into bed and then turned to Tallman. He stood and moved forward with no hesitation. The girl swiftly undressed him, laying aside coat and shirt, boots and trousers. His shoulder holster and sleeve rig were removed without comment and gently placed on the table. At last, she pulled his shorts down and murmured appreciatively as his manhood stiffened, erect and swollen. He chuckled softly and climbed into bed with Vivian.

The girl disrobed with doelike grace. She stepped out of the kimono and daintily let it drop to the floor. Her body was sleek, with lovely pink-tipped breasts, rounded hips and exquisite legs. Her pubic mound was shaved bare, the fold of her vulva visible between her thighs. She looked like a bronzed Venus.

"Ash?" Vivian's gaze was fastened on the girl. "Is she . . . staying?"

"No rules here, Viv. Let yourself go—enjoy."

Tallman kissed her before she could reply. He ran his hand up her flank and across the swell of her breasts. Then the bed jiggled and the girl slipped between Vivian's legs. He shifted, and as his mouth closed over one of her breasts, the girl's tongue traced an invisible line up her thigh. She gasped, and then, suddenly, a flood of pure sensation rippled through her body. His tongue teased her nipple erect and the girl's tongue darted quickly into her luxurious bush. He sucked and tantalized, all of her breast within his mouth, and the tip of the girl's tongue flicked faster, found the magic nub within the lips of her vulva. A low cry spiraled from her throat and her eyes were transfixed in space. Her back arched, moving to meet the girl's tongue, and a mask of unendurable pain touched her features. Her mouth opened in an agonized moan.

The girl instantly scooted away, moving to the foot of the bed. Vivian's thighs were still parted wide, her eyes heavy-lidded and her breathing ragged with passion. He swung into position, kneeling between her legs, and spread the damp fold of her muff with one hand. His other hand gripped his cock and he gently rubbed the head back and forth over the node of her clitoris. Her buttocks lifted off the bed, her eyes feverish and begging, and a long exhalation wracked her body. Her arms went out to him, her face twisted in a look of desperation, and she whispered his name over and over again in an imploring litany. He inserted the head of his shaft and wiggled it round and round within her moist cleft. Her breasts heaved with a soundless whimper and she seized his shoulders in a frantic clawhold. He drove the hard length of himself to the very wellspring of her chalice.

Vivian screamed and her legs spidered around his back. He still knelt upright and he grasped the globes of her bottom, hoisting her completely off the bed, her loins locked against his groin. The girl, positioned directly behind him, turned onto her back, wedging her head between the fork of his legs, and began laving his balls with her tongue. Vivian clung to him, her eyes shut tight and her hips bucking wildly. He dipped deep inside her and slowly withdrew, guiding her with his hands to control the rhythm of their thrusts. Her mouth closed on his with sobbing urgency and she trembled violently as she peaked and broke through the barrier. He met the upward slam of her hips and a raw jolt of power surged up the base of his spine. She spiked his shoulder muscles with her nails and the girl took his balls in her mouth, her tongue fluttering like butterfly wings. He exploded, flooding Vivian with fiery come, and her legs scissored him in a frenzied contraction. Her head arched back in a muted cry of delirium.

Lowering her, he brushed her lips with a kiss and stared tenderly into her eyes. Then he rolled onto his back and lay spread-eagled on the bed. He was still erect, and his cock towered like a colossal scepter. The girl moved between his legs and her tongue performed a sinuous dance along the length of his shaft. For an instant, Vivian was mesmerized, watching as the girl licked and teased and finally engulfed the whole of him within her mouth. A wounded look crossed Vivian's features, as though she was somehow excluded and no longer partner to the union. Abruptly, his arm went around her waist and he pulled her into a close embrace. He smiled and kissed her, gently bit her lip, and then directed her gaze downward. She saw the girl pause and swirl the head of his cock with her tongue. With feline grace, the girl then straddled him, her almond-shaped eyes wide and expectant, and sat down. His staff vanished into the bare, slippery fold of her pubis.

The girl sat perfectly still for a moment. Her taut buttocks bunched tight and she squeezed down, holding him entrapped within her warm haven. Her nipples were hard and pointed and her eyes glistened with kittenish lust. Then her hips writhed and she began moving round and round in a circular motion. The sight of her pumping on him kindled a mounting excitement in Vivian. She took one of his teats in her mouth and suckled, felt it stiffen. Her hand unwittingly went to her clitoris and she massaged herself while she watched his cock appear and disappear into the girl's mound. His haunches rose upward in harmony with the girl's downward plunge, and they joined in a clash that steadily quickened. The girl's eyes closed and her mouth sagged open and she humped faster and faster. He rammed to the core and burst inside her and she climaxed as Vivian brought herself across the threshold. The bed shook with their simultaneous eruptions and their voices were raised in a chorus of ululating groans. Then, as one, the three of them went limp.

Their bodies warm and their legs intertwined, they floated on a quenched flame. Vivian was nestled deep in the hollow of one shoulder, and on his opposite side, the girl pillowed her head against his chest. His arms pressed them tight and their breasts were softly cuddled on his hard frame. He stroked their buttocks, kissing first one and then the other, and there was a natural intimacy to their nakedness. Time lost measure and meaning, and some while later the girl drifted into a childlike sleep. Then a velvety breath eddied through the hair on his chest and he glanced around. Vivian snuggled closer, her mouth to his ear in a throaty whisper.

"Ash."

"Ummm?"

"You're a devil."

"Any regrets?"

"Only one."

"What's that?"

"It ended too soon."

"Shall we awaken our friend and start again?"

"Let me."

Vivian slipped from his embrace and knelt between his legs. Her hand went to the girl's bare cleft and her finger explored the inner wetness. Her tongue swathed the underside of his balls and then moved upward. Her eyes sparkled with a mischievous look and she caressed him with the Chinese butterfly flutter.

His cock stood straight and tall.

EIGHTEEN

Sunset cast a ruddy haze across the Fresno depot. The locomotive slowed as the engineer throttled down and set the brakes. Belching steam and smoke, the train ground to a halt.

Tallman stepped off the lead passenger coach. Three days had elapsed since his meeting with Otis Blackburn. In that time, he had dropped Vivian off at Fresno, instructing her to engage a hotel suite. Then he'd continued on to Bakersfield, and once more assumed the guise of Edmund Scott. Late the night before, he had burglarized the offices of the Kern County Land & Development Company. Over the years he had been tutored by some of the best safecrackers and yegg-men in the business, so he'd encountered no problem in breaking into Ordway's private safe. Afterwards with certain documents in his possession, he had wired Blackburn. In the morning, he'd boarded the train for Fresno, and now he was hurrying toward the hotel. Time was running short.

Vivian greeted him with a kiss and a look of avid curiosity. The suite was large and handsomely appointed, and she quickly sat him down on the sofa. Then she demanded a full accounting of his clandestine mission to Bakersfield. He touched briefly on the burglary, and spread the documents before her on a coffee table. The most damaging of the lot was a batch of letters addressed to Harlan Ordway and bearing the signature of key officials of the Santa Fe Railroad. The correspondence was incontrovertible proof that Ordway had conspired to open a new transcontinental route. A survey map indicated that Bakersfield was to be the terminus for the line. There was also a contract in which the Santa Fe agreed to purchase right-of-way across Ordway's land. The price was a thousand dollars per acre.

"So much for Ordway," Tallman concluded. "We've got him by the short hairs and no way he'll wiggle out of an indictment."

"Where do we go from here?"

"I wired Blackburn," Tallman said quietly. "Sheriff Wilcox and his thugs are due here any minute."

"I see." Vivian's voice was barely audible. "Then you're going to stick to Blackburn's plan?"

"Yes and no." Tallman kept his tone light. "I'll figure some way to burst McQuade's balloon. But I won't let the settlers take the fall with him."

"What about me?" Vivian protested. "I haven't heard anything about my part."

Tallman laughed indulgently. "I go, you stay. Your job's to hole up in this suite and guard the evidence. That way I'll know it's safe and sound."

Vivian lifted her chin defiantly. "Why do I have to sit on my duff while you have all the fun?"

"Because I'm still calling the shots, that's why."

A knock stifled her objection before it began. Tallman stuffed the documents under the sofa cushion and walked to the door. In the hallway, Sheriff Isaac Wilcox was flanked by two men. Tallman admitted them and there was a quick round of introductions. One of the men was named Luther Crow and the other was Earl Hart.

Tallman felt a chill settle over him. Crow was whipcord lean, with angular features and a cold tinsel glitter to his stare. Hart was short and chunky, with a blank expression and opaque, lusterless eyes. Both men looked tough as whang leather, and he sensed he was in the presence of assassins. Neither of them paid any attention to Vivian, and that merely heightened his concern. He motioned them to chairs and took a seat on the sofa.

"Well, Sheriff." He smiled without warmth. "We meet under better circumstances. Last time you were bound and determined to charge me with murder."

"Blackburn should've told me," Wilcox said with a hangdog look. "I only found out you was operatin' undercover when Crow gave me the lowdown. Helluva way to run a railroad!"

"So who's in charge?" Tallman inquired. "Blackburn led me to believe you were handling things."

"Oh, I am," Wilcox said, stealing a glance at Crow. "I got it laid out pretty as you please."

"Suppose you lay it out for me."

Wilcox bobbed his head. "There's two parts to it, and they've got to come off like clockwork. Your job's to get all them farmers in one place at one time. Shouldn't be too hard, what with you being their lawyer. Work up some phony excuse to call a League meetin'."

"Do you have a specific time in mind?"

"Somewheres along about noontime."

"Why so early?"

"That's the other part." Wilcox gestured at the two men. "These gents go to work the minute you've got them dirt-kickers together. They're gonna take possession of Wally Branden's farm."

"Very clever, Sheriff." Tallman's expression was sphin-xlike. "I create a diversion while you serve the eviction papers. Afterwards, Crow and Hart occupy the farm all nice and legal. What then?"

Wilcox gave him the fish-eye. "I don't get your drift."

"Let me rephrase it," Tallman said evenly. "What purpose does it serve to evict only one farmer?"

"Not your concern." Wilcox spoke like his jaws were wired shut. "We're all on the railroad's payroll and orders are orders. We do what we're told."

"Indeed we do." Tallman nodded thoughtfully. "But why noontime, Sheriff? Why not sometime after dark? Wouldn't that increase the element of surprise?"

"Looky here now—"

"Button your lip!" Crow cut him short. "You done told him all he needs to know and that's that."

Tallman turned his head just far enough to rivet Crow with a look. "Perhaps I should address my questions to you."

Crow's lips barely moved. "You got all the answers you're gonna get."

"Not quite." Tallman's gaze was pale and very direct.

"Unless I'm wrong, Blackburn sent you here to provoke a showdown. That's why you've rigged it to happen during daylight. You don't want those farmers storming the Branden place in the dark. Correct?"

"So what?" Crow's mouth zigzagged in a cruel grimace. "A few dead sodbusters ought to convince everybody we mean business."

"Wrong," Tallman said deliberately. "I won't be a party to the death of innocent people. Especially when they've been tricked into breaking the law."

Crow barked a sharp, short laugh. "Then stay the hell away, Mr. Detective. We'll sucker 'em out to the farm and you arrange to make yourself scarce. That way you don't get your hands dirty."

"No," Tallman said, steel underlying his quiet tone. "There's to be no killing. I won't allow it to happen."

"Yeah?" Crow said viciously. "How do you plan to stop it?"

Tallman's eyes hardened to slate gray. "I could refuse to call the League meeting. Then you'd have no crowd and no showdown." He paused, and his voice dropped. "Or maybe I'll just stop you."

"What makes you think you could punch my ticket?"

"Try me and see."

There was a moment of calculation while Crow studied him. Tallman stared him straight in the eye, challenging him with a look of undisguised hostility. At last, his jawline set in a scowl, the gunman shrugged.

"I'll meet you halfway," he said grudgingly. "If them farmers don't start trouble, then there won't be none. How's that sound?"

"Try fooling me," Tallman warned him, "and the joke's on you. Any attempt to antagonize those farmers and I'll personally take a hand. Understood?"

"Don't push it," Crow said with a corrosive glare. "I heard you the first time."

"Well, now!" Wilcox laughed nervously and bounded to his feet. "I reckon we're all set to go. You do your part and we'll do ours, Mr. Tallman. A little teamwork and everybody comes out smellin' like roses."

Tallman showed them to the door. The three men trooped out and disappeared down the hall. When he turned back into the room, he looked abstracted, lost in thought. Vivian finally broke the silence.

"You don't trust him, do you?"

"No," Tallman said hollowly. "He's been hired to kill and any pretext will do. I'd say it's a toss-up as to whether he keeps his word."

"But he backed off," Vivian insisted. "Won't he remember your threat tomorrow?"

"Crow doesn't scare," Tallman told her. "Cold-blooded killers always believe they've been invested with a sort of bullet-proof immortality. He pretended to compromise only because he needs me to call a League meeting. What happens when push comes to shove is anybody's guess."

"So how do you avoid bloodshed?"

"I'll do my damnedest to hold those farmers in check."

"Lots of luck," Vivian said, anguish in her eyes. "And if Crow starts the trouble himself?"

"Then I'll stop him."

"How?"

Tallman smiled. "In Crow's own inimitable lingo . . . I'll punch his ticket."

"You say that like you're bullet proof yourself!"

"On the contrary," Tallman said with a broad wink. "I have no desire to shuffle off this mortal coil. Don't be a worrywart."

"Who, me?" Vivian deadpanned. "Why should I worry?"

"Why indeed?"

"Just do me a favor, lover."

"Anything."

"Shoot first and take damn good aim!"

"I thought you knew." Tallman leaned down and kissed the vee between her breasts. "I always hit the mark."

Vivian melted in his arms. She hugged him tightly around the neck and buried her face in his shoulder. A tear rolled down her cheek like a dewdrop on pale satin.

The Hanford hotel swarmed with farmers. Some thirty League members were already in the ballroom and more were arriving by the minute. There was a pent-up air of excitement in the room and all eyes were fixed on the speaker's table. The murmur of conversation subsided as Major McQuade brought the meeting to order.

Tallman and Angela Pryor were seated at the table. Before dawn, once more in the guise of Alex Fitzhugh, he'd rousted McQuade out of bed. Talking fast, he had spun a wild tale about his trip to Sacramento. McQuade swallowed it whole and quickly agreed to call an emergency meeting. Messengers were dispatched, with instructions to have everyone in town by high noon. Now, on the edge of their seats, the crowd waited to hear what their lawyer had unearthed. McQuade kept his remarks short, and turned the floor over to Tallman. There was hushed silence as he rose to his feet.

"Good news!" He shook his fist in the air. "We've got the straight dope on the octopus—at last!"

"Whooeee!"

"Atta boy, Alex!" Wally Branden yelled. "We knew you'd do it!"

"Gawddamn, let the man talk!"

"Yeah, everybody pipe down!"

Tallman stilled them with upraised hands. "I'm sorry my trip took so long. But I think you'll agree it was worth the wait. I now have proof positive that the land grants were transferred to the Southern Pacific only one week— *one week*—before you were served with eviction notices. You've been hoodwinked!"

"Praise the Lord!" Iver Kneutson whooped. "We're saved, boys! Saved!"

"Not only that," Tallman went on quickly, "I've located an informant in San Francisco. He wants money, but he's willing to testify that there was collusion between the railroad and the district court judge. Think of it!"

The crowd roared and Tallman beamed proudly. Everything he'd said was a pack of lies, and inside he pitied them for their gullible acceptance. Yet his greater concern was that a prolonged meeting would lead to hard questions. Timing was crucial, and he wondered how soon the sheriff would act. He put the thought aside and got on with his windy performance.

"Now here's the way—"

A shrill scream echoed through the room. Everyone turned in unison and Wally Branden jackknifed to his feet. His wife stood framed in the doorway. Her hair was disheveled and one sleeve of her gingham dress was ripped at the shoulder. She rushed forward, her voice choked with terror.

"Wally! Oh God, Wally! They've taken our farm!"

Branden grabbed her by the arms. "What're you talkin' about, Ellie? Who's taken the farm?"

"The railroad!" Ellie Branden wailed. "Sheriff Wilcox evicted us! Threw me and the kids out of our own house. Just like we was trash, Wally!"

For a moment, the crowd appeared thunderstruck. Then the farmers leaped from their chairs and a guttural roar reverberated through the room. McQuade silenced them with a sharp command and hurried around the speaker's table. He halted before Ellie Branden.

"Pay attention!" he demanded. "Was Wilcox alone?"

Ellie Branden shook her head. "He's got two men with him. Told me they represented the railroad and they'd come to repossess our farm. They're out there right now— in my house!"

McQuade silently blessed the gods. The opportunity he'd waited for was at hand, and he seized it. His face blazing with rage, he turned on the crowd.

"You heard her! Wilcox and those railroad stooges manhandled Ellie and her children. They've invaded our homes and our land, evicted one of our own! Are you gonna let them get away with it?"

His goad instantly transformed the farmers from a

crowd into a mob. The room shook with a collective uproar that was part fury and part bloodlust. The men surged around him, their faces contorted and their voices crying vengeance. McQuade led them storming out the door.

Tallman left Angela Pryor to look after the Branden woman. Then he hurried along in the wake of the crowd. He thought it ironic that the railroad's move played directly into the hands of McQuade and Harlan Ordway. The farmers were mobilized and on the warpath, the very thing McQuade had been unable to accomplish over the past year. He wondered how he could stop men who were now hellbent on getting themselves killed. And somehow, as though predestined, he knew how it would end.

He would be forced to kill Luther Crow.

The day was bright as new brass, without a cloud in the sky. Sheriff Isaac Wilcox, shaded from the sun, stood on the farmhouse porch. He was flanked by Crow on one side and Hart on the other, both men cradling double-barreled shotguns in their arms. The hammers were earred back to full-cock.

McQuade and the farmers halted their wagons on the road. Climbing down, they bunched together in a tight phalanx and walked toward the house. Wally Branden and Iver Kneutson were in the front rank, matching McQuade stride for stride. Tallman eased off to one side, and took up a vantage point on the edge of the crowd. A few yards from the porch, McQuade threw up his arm. The farmers stopped in a shoulder-to-shoulder wedge.

"Wilcox!" McQuade thundered. "You've overstepped

your bounds. Take your thugs and get the hell out of here!"

"You're a mite confused," Wilcox said harshly. "I'm here on official business and I've got a court order that says it's legal."

"Damn your court order!" McQuade bellowed. "We won't be rawhided off our land by the Southern Pacific or anybody else. You've got ten seconds to move out or else we'll move you!"

"Go ahead and try," Wilcox countered. "As sheriff, I'm sworn to uphold the law. I mean to do just that, Major."

Crow and Hart lowered the muzzles of their shotguns. The bores looked like mine shafts at close range, and the crowd froze in a stilled tableau. An oppressive sense of violence settled over the farmyard and everyone seemed to hold their breath. Tallman abruptly took a step away from the farmers and faced them with upraised palms.

"Hold it!" he called out. "The railroad wants you to use force. Open your eyes and take a look. It's a setup, a trap! These men were sent here to kill you."

"Stay out of it!" McQuade gave him a dirty look. "We're here and we won't back down!"

"Listen to me!" Tallman directed his attention to the farmers. "A piece of land isn't worth dying over! You'll only get yourselves—"

"Don't shoot!"

Crow's panicky shout rang out across the farmyard. He leveled a forefinger, pointing toward the rear of the crowd. Stunned by the outburst, everyone instinctively turned to look. The instant their eyes left him, Crow triggered both barrels on his shotgun.

A hailstorm of buckshot whistled into the crowd.

Wally Branden and Iver Kneutson were knocked off their feet. Several other farmers doubled over and dropped to the ground. Of those in the front rank, only McQuade went unscathed. A single ball plucked at his sleeve and struck a farmer behind him.

All thought suspended, Tallman acted on reflex alone. His arm moved and the Colt appeared in his hand. He drew a bead on Crow and fired two quick shots. The slugs impacted beneath the breastbone and jerked the gunman off the porch like a haywire puppet. His arms flailed in a nerveless dance and the shotgun slipped from his grasp. He pitched raglike on the ground.

McQuade and the sheriff pulled their pistols almost simultaneously. A split second before either of them cleared leather, Hart let loose with his scattergun. Behind twin sheets of flame, the barrels vomited a double load of buckshot. The blast winnowed the ranks of the farmers like a giant scythe. Three men were hurled backward, splattered with blood and gore, and collapsed without a sound. Another farmer clutched his throat, a crimson fountain spurting through his fingers, and staggered a few steps before he slumped face down in the dirt. McQuade, by some miraculous fluke, was again untouched.

Isaac Wilcox lost his nerve in the clutch. He thumbed off a hurried snap-shot and saw it kick up a puff of dust at McQuade's feet. His hand shook violently as he fought to align the sights for a second shot. McQuade coolly extended his pistol at arm's length and fired. The slug splintered Wilcox's collarbone and slammed him up against the side of the house. McQuade took deliberate aim and shot him in the heart. The sheriff slumped to his knees and toppled over like a felled tree.

A step away, Hart tossed the shotgun aside and clawed at a pistol stuck in his waistband. His eyes swung to Tallman as he brought the six-gun out and thumbed the hammer. Tallman sighted over the top of the barrel and the Colt spat twice in a staccato roar. The explosive bullets blew a gaping hole in Hart's shirtfront. He hit the porch and somersaulted, landing with his head crooked at an odd angle. His opaque eyes stared sightlessly.

Tallman lowered the Colt. A haze of gunsmoke hung over the farmyard, and all around him was carnage and death. The bloodbath he'd tried to avoid was evident wherever he looked. He counted nine farmers down, many of them already dead and others grievously wounded. Added to the sheriff and the two gunmen, it gave the scene the look of a battlefield. Yet the stench of voided bowels, mixed with the sweet smell of blood, conjured forth another image entirely. He was reminded of a slaughterhouse. A killing ground slippery with offal.

Then, slowly, his gaze shifted to McQuade. At the very forefront of the fight, the major hadn't suffered so much as a scratch. Tallman idly wondered if he led a charmed life. But the thought was fleeting; no man lived beyond his appointed time, McQuade included. Nor was he unkillable. Instead, this was something more on the order of a reprieve. A stay of execution.

Tallman resolved it would be a short one.

NINETEEN

Funeral services were held next morning. By nine o'clock the street outside the Methodist church was swamped with people. All of Hanford turned out in a public show of support for the League.

The church was filled to capacity with an overflow spilling out onto the steps. Four coffins, draped with sprays of wild flowers, were aligned before the altar. The wives and children of the slain farmers were seated in pews down front. Behind them were McQuade and the remaining members of the League. Tallman sat beside Angela Pryor.

The preacher delivered a stirring eulogy. Attired in a hammertail coat, he praised the deceased as good Christians and devoted family men, struck down in the prime of life. The one consolation, almost a miracle he noted, was that more men had not died. The five other farmers wounded in yesterday's shootout would apparently survive their wounds. He then raised his fist to heaven and beseeched the Lord God Jehovah to smite the Southern Pacific Railroad. His eye-for-an-eye invocation reflected the general mood of the crowd.

League members, six to a coffin, acted as pallbearers. The mourners fell in behind, their faces tear-streaked and their sobs loud in the still morning air. Outside the church the cortege proceeded to a cemetery on the edge of town. Angela, weepy-eyed in her black crepe dress, clung to Tallman's arm. At graveside, the coffins were lowered on to planks laid across freshly dug holes. Onlookers were packed row upon row, with immediate family huddled forlornly around the coffins. The preacher opened his Bible and began reading in a sepulchral voice.

"The Lord is my shepherd; I shall not want. He maketh me to lie down in green pastures. He leadeth . . ."

Tallman scarcely heard the words. His eyes were empty and cold in the bright sunlight. He was aware of Angela sniffling at his side and he supported her with an arm around her shoulder. Yet his mind was fixed on Major Thomas McQuade. Overnight he had devoted considerable thought to the problem. He saw only one recourse, and while it was extreme, there seemed no alternative. Arrest and imprisonment, in his view, was not fitting retribution for a Judas. At last, determined to exact harsher punishment, he decided to wait until after the graveside services. He wanted a public spectacle that would capture headlines. And an open admission of guilt.

". . . with the certainty that we shall all meet again at the Resurrection, through Jesus Christ our Lord. Amen."

The prayer ended with a leaden moment of silence. Then the pallbearers moved forward to lower the coffins into the ground. Tallman stepped out of the crowd and halted before the graves. He motioned the pallbearers aside and turned. His voice rang out across the cemetery.

"We have unfinished business here! Before we lay these men to rest, I think everyone should know the true identity of their murderer. Sheriff Wilcox and those railroad goons were merely the instrument of their death. The man who actually got them killed stands here among you today. His name is Thomas McQuade!"

A gruff buzz of outrage swept through the crowd. All eyes turned to McQuade, and several farmers, as though to protect him, quickly joined ranks. His features were set in a grim scowl.

"Have you lost your mind, Fitzhugh?"

"We'll soon find out." Tallman gave him a sardonic smile. "Does the name Harlan Ordway ring any bells, Major?"

A fleeting look of puzzlement crossed McQuade's face, then his expression became flat and guarded. "I don't know what you're talking about."

"Do you deny that you are in Ordway's employ?"

"I most certainly do!"

"Do you deny that Ordway sent you to Hanford?"

"You're off your rocker!"

"Isn't it true you were ordered here to organize the Settlers' League and foster hostility with the railroad?"

"That's a lie!" McQuade's eyes burned with intensity. "And you're a scurrilous liar, Fitzhugh!"

Tallman regarded him with a level gaze. "I suppose it's also a lie that you were responsible for the Southern Pacific bombings?"

"Every word of it!" McQuade shouted. "All a pack of lies!"

"Come, come, Major." Tallman's voice was alive with

contempt. "The blood of these dead men is on your hands. Are you asking us to believe otherwise?"

"I'm not asking," McQuade said, his eyes garnet with rage. "I'm telling you to back off or suffer the consequences. I will not tolerate your false accusations any further!"

"How about proof?" Tallman fished a slip of paper from his inside coat pocket. "I have here a letter from the Santa Fe Railroad to Harlan Ordway. It proves beyond question that a conspiracy existed to establish a new transcontinental route. Does that refresh your memory, Major?"

McQuade went rock still. "I'm warning you for the last time."

"Save your breath," Tallman said, his jaw set in a hard line. "This letter proves the Settlers' League was organized for one purpose and one purpose only. The goal was to divert attention from the Santa Fe by turning the spotlight on the League. And that's why you were sent to Hanford."

"It proves nothing!" McQuade's mouth clamped in a bloodless slit. "Not where I'm concerned anyway. I've had no dealings with Ordway or the Santa Fe!"

"On the contrary." Tallman pretended to read the letter. "It says here, and I quote directly, 'Advise McQuade to intensify his efforts. We dare not proceed until he has the Settlers' League embroiled in an all out war with the Southern Pacific.' I'd call that proof positive, in black and white. Would you care to comment, Major?"

A vein pulsed in McQuade's forehead. His face was rigid and his eyes blazed with fury. An instant slipped past while they stared at one another. Then his hand snaked inside his coat.

Tallman seemed to move not at all. The Colt appeared out of nowhere and he fired as McQuade's pistol cleared leather. McQuade stood perfectly still, a great bloodburst spattered across the breast of his coat. His mouth worked in soundless amazement and he triggered a shot into the dirt. Then his eyes rolled back in his head and his knees buckled. He fell dead.

Silence descended on the graveyard. The farmers stared at the body with looks of stunned shock. No one spoke, and none of them seemed able to comprehend the suddenness of McQuade's death. Then Tallman holstered his Colt and the movement broke their spell. He held the letter aloft.

"Use this in your fight with the Southern Pacific! It clears you of any part in the conspiracy and it proves you had no hand in the sabotage. I suggest you make it available to newspapers throughout the state. Let the press tell your side of the story for a change!"

"Hold on!" one of the farmers said. "You sound like you ain't gonna stick around. If the Major was everything you claim, then our fat's not out of the fire yet. We'll need your help more'n ever!"

"No," Tallman assured him. "All you need is this letter and somebody to get the newshounds together. I'll leave it with Angela Pryor. She knows all the details and she's got a way with words—and she's certain to draw a crowd."

The comment drew smiles and nods of approval. Tallman quit while he was ahead, and gave Angela the high sign. She took his arm and they made their way out of the cemetery. The crowd milled around in some confusion, watching as they turned at the church and walked toward town. A moment later they disappeared from view.

On Main Street, Tallman stopped in front of the hotel. He handed Angela the letter and waited while she slowly read it. She appeared surprised and somewhat taken aback. Then she smiled an upside down smile.

"There's no mention of McQuade in here."

"I improvised." Tallman's expression was stoic. "After yesterday, I figured the punishment ought to fit the crime."

"So you tricked him . . . and killed him."

"I gave him a chance to kill me. You might say he committed suicide by trying."

"Who are you?" Angela asked in a small voice. "I know you're not a lawyer. Are you a lawman of some kind?"

"Who I am isn't all that important. So let's just say I'm a fellow passing through. Here today and gone tomorrow."

"No," Angela corrected him. "You'll be gone today, won't you?"

Tallman smiled. "Not without fond memories."

"Will I ever see you again?"

"Who knows when our paths might cross?"

Angela caught his eye for an instant, looked quickly away. "I hate to see you leave without a proper good-bye. Maybe I could come up to your room and help you . . . pack."

"A tempting offer."

"One good turn deserves another. And we're all in your debt."

"Are you speaking for the League or yourself?"

"I'll let you decide when we get upstairs."

"Unfortunately," Tallman said, consulting his pocket-watch, "time grows short. I have to catch the ten o'clock northbound."

"Well, then," Angela replied with a sudden sad grin, "shall we call it one for the road? A momento of your stopover in Hanford."

"How long a momento do you have in mind?"

"We'll never know till we try."

Angela hugged his arm to her breast and they entered the hotel. Upstairs she waited until the door was closed and then stretched herself out across the bed. She lifted her skirts and showed him why it wouldn't take long. Her momento was bare.

Tallman made his train with only seconds to spare.

TWENTY

A blistering midday sun beat down on Chicago's Loop district. The noon hour was drawing to a close and Washington Street was crowded with office workers returning from lunch. A hansom cab pulled to curbside and stopped.

Tallman stepped down from the cab. He was attired in a powder gray single-breasted suit, with a charcoal gray tie and a matching pocket handkerchief. The brim of his fedora was sloped at a roguish curve and added a certain panache to his appearance. He looked rested and relaxed, and his expression was one of high good humor. He slipped the driver a ten spot and entered the office building at a brisk stride.

Upstairs, Tallman walked directly to the door of the Pinkerton Agency. The receptionist looked up as he moved into the outer office. Her eyes went big and round, and her mouth ovaled in a silent gasp. He swept his fedora off with an eloquent gesture.

"Good afternoon, Myrna."

"Mr. Tallman!"

"Were you expecting someone else?"

"No, it's just—" Myrna stammered, then went on in a rush. "You were reported missing almost a week ago. Mr. Pinkerton's absolutely beside himself!"

Tallman smiled. "I was delayed en route."

"Watch yourself," Myrna whispered softly. "He's hopping mad."

"I appreciate the tip. And allow me to say you've never looked more ravishing."

Myrna's Kewpie-doll features turned scarlet. "Anytime you have a free evening . . ."

"I'll treasure the thought."

Tallman gave her a sly wink and hooked his fedora on a halltree. Before she could move, he swiftly crossed the room. He opened the door to Pinkerton's office and walked in with an air of hearty good cheer.

"The prodigal returns! How are you, boss?"

Pinkerton's look could have drawn blood. He slowly replaced his pen in an inkwell and pushed a stack of papers aside. Then he waited while Tallman approached the desk and seated himself in an armchair. Neither of them offered to shake hands.

"You might have wired me," Pinkerton said stiffly. "I've had agents turning California upside down searching for you."

"I'm flattered you went to so much trouble."

"Where have you been?"

"Chinatown."

"Chinatown?" Pinkerton eyed him narrowly. "Is that some sort of joke?"

"Like the fly walking across the mirror said"—Tallman

paused and spread his hands—"it all depends on how you look at it."

"Your humor escapes me."

"Nobody's perfect."

"Very amusing," Pinkerton grunted. "I want some answers, Ash. And I won't be fobbed off with wisecracks!"

"Fire away."

"Why did you leave California?" Pinkerton demanded. "Your orders were to report to Otis Blackburn."

"I have nothing to say to Blackburn."

"Well, he had a great deal to say about you."

Tallman chuckled. "I wouldn't be at all surprised."

"I received a five-page telegram from Blackburn. Among other things, he accuses you of purposely aborting your assignment."

"No truth to it, boss."

"Indeed?" Pinkerton huffed. "I understand you killed a man by the name of McQuade?"

"Guilty as charged."

"May I inquire the reason?"

"A personal idiosyncrasy," Tallman said genially. "When someone points a gun at me, I have an overpowering urge to shoot first. It's a hard habit to break."

Pinkerton stared at him. "I am reliably informed that you goaded the man into pulling his gun."

"Don't believe everything Blackburn says."

"He also informs that McQuade was the key witness in the case."

"I won't deny that."

"So it's true!" Pinkerton snorted. "You killed the one man who could have exposed the conspirators. The *only* man we might reasonably have expected to turn state's evidence!"

"Not so," Tallman said equably. "McQuade was no canary. He'd have cut his own tongue out before he turned songbird."

"Is that why you killed him?"

"I've already explained—"

"Please!" Pinkerton interrupted. "I would appreciate a candid answer. Your real reason."

Tallman's mouth hardened and he was silent for a time. When at last he spoke, the words were clipped and brittle. "Forget about Blackburn and McQuade being on opposite sides of the fence. For all practical purposes, they were working toward the same end. Both of them were determined to provoke a showdown and somehow use it to fuel the fire. As you know, they finally got their wish. And the upshot was that four good men died needless deaths."

"Four?" Pinkerton repeated. "The number I heard was seven."

"The sheriff and those two gunmen don't count. Whatever they got was less than they deserved."

"You're a hard man, Ash."

"I don't approve of hired assassins."

"Nor do I," Pinkerton said in a resonant voice. "However, to return to McQuade. You killed him because he led those farmers to their deaths. Is that correct?"

"I found it reason enough." Tallman permitted himself a grim smile. "In fact, if Blackburn had been there that day, I might have killed him too. He was just as culpable as McQuade."

"Perhaps you're overly harsh in your judgment of Blackburn."

"Harsh but not unfair," Tallman said coolly. "Any man who hires assassins is by definition an assassin himself."

Pinkerton tried another tack. "I understand you acquired certain evidence on the major conspirator, Harlan Ordway?"

"I wired Blackburn to that effect."

"May I ask you how you came into possession of the evidence?"

Tallman's wooden expression cracked with a slight smile. "Let's just say I obtained it. How doesn't really matter."

"Very well." Pinkerton watched him intently. "What form does this evidence take?"

"Documents," Tallman replied. "Solid proof that Ordway and the Santa Fe were involved in a covert railroad scheme."

"Do these documents implicate the Santa Fe in the conspiracy?"

"You mean the bombings and the farmers' revolt?"

"Yes."

"Not really," Tallman commented. "I tend to believe Ordway organized all that on his own. Whether or not the Santa Fe was aware of it . . . we'll probably never know."

Pinkerton studied him a moment, then finally nodded. "How damaging are the documents? Would public disclosure of their contents stop the Santa Fe from extending track into California?"

"No question about it."

"And Ordway?" Pinkerton persisted. "Would the documents secure a criminal indictment against him?"

"Indictment and conviction," Tallman elaborated. "At the very least, he'd spend the rest of his life in prison."

"Where are these documents now?"

"I have them in safekeeping."

"Which means you have no intention of surrendering them voluntarily?"

"None at all."

Pinkerton raised his leonine head and glowered across the desk. "I won't bore you with threats. You're aware that I could ruin you professionally. A word dropped here and there and you would be unemployable as a detective." He paused, let the tension build. "In short, I could quite easily transform you into a pariah. An outcast."

"Perhaps," Tallman observed dryly. "But that wouldn't serve the best interests of your client. And with all due modesty, it would also rob you of my indispensable services. Are you willing to go that far?"

"Confound you, Ash!" Pinkerton let go a wheezy sort of chuckle. "You're a brazen scoundrel. And one of these days—"

"But not today."

"No, not today," Pinkerton conceded. "As an alternative to booting you out, what would you suggest?"

"We negotiate." Tallman grinned broadly. "I suspect Blackburn's already authorized you to act on behalf of the Southern Pacific?"

"What are your terms?"

"Quite simple." Tallman busied himself lighting a cigar. "I'll surrender the documents and provide a sworn deposition for the grand jury. Ordway goes to prison and the Santa Fe gets left in the lurch."

"And in return?"

"The Southern Pacific deeds the land over to the settlers. No strings, no tricks—a clear, unencumbered deed."

"I'm not sure Blackburn will bend that far."

"I am," Tallman said with conviction. "Otherwise he'll lose all of southern California to the Santa Fe. By comparison, the farmers in Hanford are small potatoes."

Pinkerton deliberated briefly, then shrugged. "Very well, your terms are acceptable. How soon can you produce the documents?"

"The minute I see a transfer agreement—signed and duly executed—awarding deed to the settlers."

"Aren't you being a tad too cynical?"

"Not where Otis Blackburn's concerned."

"It's an imperfect world," Pinkerton noted. "Only a fine line separates saints from sinners."

"So where does that leave us?"

"Certainly not on the side of the sinners!"

"I'll take your word for it, chief."

Tallman stuck the cigar in his mouth and stood. He waved with a chipper grin and walked out the door, trailing a laugh and a cloud of smoke. Pinkerton stared at the door, wondering not for the first time why the unruly ones always made the best detectives. He shook his head and went back to work.

The house was on the outskirts of Chicago. A stone dwelling secluded in a grove of trees, it was Tallman's private hideaway. His associates, Allan Pinkerton included, were unaware of its existence. He shared the secret with only one other person.

Tallman entered the foyer and walked toward the parlor door. Without warning, Vivian slithered around the corner and greeted him with a seductive smile. She was scantily clad in a garter belt and black net stockings and high-topped red leather boots. Her breasts were bare and her auburn hair hung long and unbound. She laughed and held out a bottle of champagne.

"Merry Christmas!"

Tallman grinned. "Saint Nick isn't due for six months or so."

"Happy birthday?" she giggled. "Trick or treat? Any excuse will do for me."

"What's the occasion?"

"We're celebrating!" She raised the bottle overhead. "Here's to our first case together . . . and whatever the future may bring!"

Tallman inspected her costume. "Where's your whip?"

"Who needs a whip?" She vamped him with a look. "You've got something better to flog me with, lover!"

"Well, then," Tallman nodded archly, "prepare to be flogged."

"You devil!" She struck a pose. "Like my surprise?"

"A good deal more than I expected," he said, eyeing her hungrily.

"Ooooh!" she purred. "You look good enough to eat."

"Come to think of it, I'm getting hungry myself."

Tallman laughed and spread his arms wide. Her breasts jiggled and her auburn muff wig-wagged beneath the garter belt as she hurried across the foyer. He swept her up in a tight embrace and kissed her long and tenderly. Then he led her toward the bedroom.

The champagne was gone in an hour. The meal lasted all night.